WOMBAT CREEK

Single mother Summer Dalton arrives from New South Wales to her grandfather's small farm in the Western District. However, memories of her hippy parents' banishment for their free-loving morals — decades before — remain. Her hope is to settle on the land she's inherited, so she refuses her new neighbour Ethan Bourke's offer to buy her out. Then, a jealous old flame and Ethan's disapproving mother come into the mix. Can Summer and Ethan resolve their growing attraction to one another?

Books by Noelene Jenkinson
in the Linford Romance Library:

A WHIRLWIND ROMANCE
OUTBACK HERO
STARTING AGAIN
OCEAN BLUE
NANNY WANTED

NOELENE JENKINSON

WOMBAT CREEK

Complete and Unabridged

LINFORD
Leicester

First published in Great Britain in 2011

First Linford Edition
published 2012

British Library CIP Data

Jenkinson, Noelene.
　Wombat Creek. - - (Linford romance library)
　1. Australia- -Fiction. 2. Love stories.
　3. Large type books.
　I. Title II. Series
　823.9′2–dc23

　ISBN 978–1–4448–1253–4

Published by
F. A. Thorpe (Publishing)
Anstey, Leicestershire

Set by Words & Graphics Ltd.
Anstey, Leicestershire
Printed and bound in Great Britain by
T. J. International Ltd., Padstow, Cornwall

This book is printed on acid-free paper

1

Ethan Bourke drove along the familiar narrow road back to his sheep stud property at Karingal Park, his mind neutral and elsewhere. One elbow rested on the open window of his dark green Range Rover and his fingers drummed on the steering wheel to the beat of country music from the radio.

As he passed the neighbouring property, Greenbanks, he was hit with a twinge of nostalgia for its former elderly owner and his lifetime friend, Amos Dalton. Ethan had regarded Amos like a grandfather, and he missed his wise words and conversation.

A glint of sun on something caught his eye as he passed. Then he noticed the rusted front gate wide open and fresh tyre tracks on the wet gravel of the unsealed lane down to the cottage. Alarm bells rang. A sign clearly marked the property as *Private, Keep Out.* He jammed his Blundstone booted foot hard on the brake. The tyres of his four-wheel drive skidded to a stop. He let out a healthy curse and felt a kick of annoyance in his gut.

'Trespassers, Brewster,' he muttered to his kelpie sheepdog sitting to attention, panting, on the front seat beside him. He'd promised Amos on what proved to be his last visit to the old man in Hamilton hospital that he'd watch out for the place. 'Let's go check it out.'

His large powerful vehicle whined as he reversed and wheeled hard right, taking the lane at impatient speed. One glimpse of the flower-painted battered Volkswagen van and he immediately thought social misfit; probably someone seeking a quiet, unoccupied place out of the way to squat and freeload.

His first instinct was to reach for the CB radio to contact the local police, then he decided to check out the situation first. A decent blast of his voice and

2

a scowl from underneath his Akubra might be enough to send the intruders hightailing it out of here and back where they came from. If they proved reasonable and moved on without a fuss, he'd do something about a more secure catch for that gate, even though it wasn't his responsibility.

★　★　★

Summer Dalton sat cross-legged in the middle of a grassy paddock sloping away from the uninhabited mud brick cottage behind. A small glistening dam snuggled into the lee of a low hill below, bouncing diamonds of reflected sunlight from its surface. She heard Wombat Creek rushing and full with winter rains as it gurgled and wound its way between banks of ferny undergrowth somewhere further down. An exhilarating breeze streamed her long dark hair back off her face and she caught her breath, allowing herself a gentle smile.

The cottage had obviously been built with the incredible view in mind. Fenced green squares of fields, white blobs of grazing sheep dotting the paddocks, an occasional house here and there, protected by a precious stand of native eucalypt bushland that had never been cleared, or others with sentinel rows of pines along perimeter fences. All of it epitomising the rich grazing landscape among the rolling hills and valleys of this area, the prosperous wool growing region of south western Victoria.

More accustomed to the humidity and lushness of a rainforest in the hinterland of northern New South Wales only a short drive from a long stretch of classic Australian coast, Summer found the refreshing wind whipping up the contours of the hillside a brisk, shivery change and tucked her long peasant skirt tighter around her ankles. She heaved a contented sigh, drew up her knees and hugged them. The hundred-acre farmlet was small enough for her to work alone and an ideal pocket of freedom to raise her four year old daughter, Ivy.

As soon as she had driven her kombi van in off the road and rounded the corner to reveal the house and its view, Summer had immediately fallen in love and decided to stay. She plucked a blade of cool grass from beside her and twirled it in her fingers. This acreage was her chance to break away, to strike out on her own and start anew.

Uneasily, she felt the cold metal shape of the large old fashioned front door key that she had just collected from the Hamilton lawyers handling her grandfather's estate when she had also set up a future appointment. The next step was to gather her courage and investigate the house. Always bold, she analysed why it bothered her.

Locked in deep thought, Summer heard the roaring vehicle approach before she saw it. Reluctantly, she dragged her gaze away from the tranquil view and pushed her tall slim frame from its grassy seat.

As she turned to investigate the visitor, the four-wheel drive ground to a sudden stop and the motor died. The door opened and was slammed shut with force. A giant of a man, beautifully proportioned, strode determinedly toward her.

He was worth getting up for! Fascinated by his easy, rolling gait and booted feet that ate up the distance between them, she admired the partly-open checked shirt and traditional cream moleskins snugly fitted to his lower body. Of course, what else would a man like this wear? The clothes and assertive walk spoke big property, old money and breeding. A wide-brimmed hat was tugged low over the forehead of his tanned face and half hid his eyes, but did not hide the down-turn of his mouth.

Summer sighed. Why would anyone, rich or poor, wear such a dark scowl on such a fabulous spring day? She surmised that it could mean only one thing. Trouble.

As he halted, towering over her, a

flicker of softness passed across his eyes. She watched him briefly struggle before he swiftly quashed it and his glare turned glacial.

Ah, she thought, *a man who hides his feelings.*

★ ★ ★

The instant his gaze landed on the young woman standing quietly confident and undaunted before him, Ethan's step faltered. She sure had a lot of nerve. Then, to his annoyance and in wilful conflict, he felt his heart rate quicken.

Tall and gracefully slender, her unique beauty momentarily stopped his planned tirade. In all conscience, how could he lecture anyone so lovely? Yet he recognised an underlying steely spirit and conviction not easily breached, revealed in that directly challenging gaze from clear, sky-blue eyes.

When his wits returned after their momentary lapse, his gaze of amazement took over. She was so young. He was surprised that the thought drew a moment of regret from him. And her loose clothes; colourful but unflattering. Unusual to say the least. A chord of connection sounded at the back of his mind but he couldn't quite decide why.

Her sapphire eyes danced in carefree mischief from beneath the brim of a large, black felt hat with a wide floppy brim. It topped a glossy stream of straight black hair that billowed down to her tiny waist. Wayward strands, teased by the afternoon breeze, veiled one cheek. The wind fluttered her long floral skirt around bare feet and ankles. With her magnificent waist-length hair and understated beauty, he couldn't stem his personal admiration. The graceful young woman sucked the breath out of him with her iridescent eyes and gentle poise.

With difficulty, he reverted his attention back to business.

'What are you doing here?' he barked.

★ ★ ★

Summer decided to humour him. She had watched with amusement as the man's critical gaze swung from prejudice to controlled disinterest.

'Resting.' It had been a long three-day drive.

'You're trespassing.'

'No,' she responded quietly. 'You are. This is my land.' She crossed her arms at the waist and stared him out, revealing the mettle that had seen her struggle to survive a fruitless five-year relationship with Ivy's father and move on as a single mother to raise her daughter alone after his desertion of them.

'Yours?' His eyebrows rose in disbelief and then creased in doubt that she might just be telling the truth.

'My grandfather, Amos Dalton, left it to me.' She extended a slender hand. 'Summer Dalton.'

His eyes widened in sudden realisation, as though some kind of connection had clicked into place. 'You're Amos' granddaughter!' A large brown hand slowly

9

reached out to grip hers. 'Ethan Bourke,' he stated with firm pride as though he expected her to identify him.

Her fingers disappeared into his grasp. His hold was rough but warm.

'You can let go now.' Judging by his serious expression, her teasing washed over him without effect, but he eased his grip and released her hand. 'Do you have another first name?'

He frowned in puzzlement. 'Why?'

They always asked that. 'Helps me with your aura,' she explained. 'The vibes I get from people. Yours is very strong.' She'd grown up among people with questioning minds who challenged the conventions of traditional society, and had always been openly intuitive.

After a moment of silent debate, he replied, 'Winslow.'

Summer smiled to herself. She regarded him steadily, letting her gaze play over the tanned face, the crinkles at the corners of his brown eyes, the confidence in his deep voice. 'Ethan Winslow Bourke,' she repeated slowly, tasting the words as she voiced them. 'Sounds very English.'

'Winslow is my mother's maiden name. Her family came from Wiltshire,' he replied awkwardly.

'It suits you.'

'Glad you approve.'

He let down his guard enough to permit the start of a wry grin. So there was a sense of humour, after all, buried way down deep.

Their verbal sparring sprang from a mutual and undeniable fascination for the other. Summer certainly felt it and saw his kindred reaction mirrored in his eyes.

Summer guessed his serious side didn't come from arrogance but an innate authority and responsibility into which he had probably been born. He would be a man you could trust with your life and the thought of that intrigued her.

'You live nearby,' she stated.

'Karingal Park.' He turned and nodded east. 'Beyond the rise.'

Summer's gaze followed the direction he indicated across grassy pastures nourishing flocks of sheep. 'Sounds aboriginal.'

'It means peaceful home. The natives used to camp here in the early days.' He paused, then explained, 'Since Amos died, I've been keeping an eye on his farm.'

That explained his unexpected visit. 'Thank you.'

Ethan lifted his broad shoulders into an easy shrug. 'I knew Amos all my life. I admired him. He was a gentleman farmer.'

Not for the first time in recent months, Summer wished she had known her grandfather. She envied Ethan's friend-ship with him and wanted to learn more. All in good time.

It was enticing to hear her grand-father so highly spoken-of when her father never mentioned him at all.

'We didn't see you at the funeral . . . ' His deep voice tailed off and rumbled with reproach.

Summer ignored the criticism and explained. 'No. When David was disowned twenty years ago, he refused to return. He and Amos were estranged and never kept in touch. Anyway, apparently there was some wording to that effect in grandfather's will.'

Summer remembered her own disappointment at having to abide by Amos' last wishes. Always short of cash, she might have sold the van to pay for the flight down and attend.

Since the lawyer's letter and her arrival at Greenbanks, she regretted the loss that felt more like deprivation.

As it was, she had only just scraped enough funds together for this trip. She had slept in the van for two uncomfortable, cramped nights to save on accommodation. But by far the hardest decision had been leaving Ivy behind with her parents until Summer investigated her inherited property to see if the house was habitable and the land viable before making any decision whether she would stay or return north.

She had no idea what to expect, but her daughter's happiness and stability always came first and was worth any sacrifice.

'You've come to arrange the sale?' Ethan cut into her thoughts.

A logical assumption. It had been a possibility until she'd seen the place. Summer shook her head.

He stabbed her a crisp glance. 'You're not selling?'

His look of disbelief made Summer dig her sandals deeper into the cool grass underfoot and stiffen her spine with resolve.

He hesitated before understanding dawned and he added, 'You plan on living here? Working the place?'

'My grandfather did.'

'But . . . you're a woman.'

'Top marks for observation,' she commented dryly.

'Are you alone?'

'For the moment.'

'This acreage is no bigger than a postage stamp.' His gaze swept the lush countryside behind her before settling

14

back on her serene face. 'Amos struggled and he was born to the land. You won't survive alone.'

'Won't I?' She stared him out. 'I don't need to make a lot of money. Lifestyle is more important to me. Small plots of land can be developed to become highly productive.'

'For what?'

'All kinds of farm produce and animals.'

He hooked his thumbs into his waistband and relaxed his stance. His gaze drifted over her as unimportant and her disappointment rose.

'What happens if your financial ends don't meet?'

'I doubt that will happen, but thank you for your concern.'

'You might end up relying on social welfare.'

'I've always supported myself.' Despite herself, Summer bristled at having to explain and defend herself in this un-dignified way.

'Unlike your father?'

Summer drew in a deeper breath of tolerance and brushed aside the strands of hair blowing over her shoulder and across her face. 'Have you ever met my father?'

'Of course not.'

'Yet you've judged him. David is a greenie like me. There's no harm in that. If everyone cared a little more about their planet, the world might be in a better place. My father has developed and run an organic farm all his life. I couldn't have learned from a better teacher. He successfully practised permaculture for decades before it became fashionable. Perhaps he could teach you a thing or two on your own property, Mr Bourke,' she mocked, stimulated by the challenge he presented.

Ethan clenched his jaw. 'I doubt it.'

She lifted one shoulder in a careless shrug and just for cheeky good measure, ran a blunt eye over him as he had done earlier to her. The trace of a smile pushed his humour to the surface again and he touched his hat in an acknowledged salute.

'Let's agree to disagree, shall we?' she said. 'And since I'm taking residence on my property from today, you don't need to bother checking on it any more. I can look after it now.'

He eyed her steadily. 'I hope so.'

She felt a twinge of disappointment at his prejudice. Summer's weariness after the long drive and worry at leaving Ivy behind suddenly fell heavily upon her like an unwelcome weight and she found herself eager for her neighbour to leave — if only to avoid any further disagreement to add to her apprehension over being a stranger coping with the unfamiliar and starting a whole new life.

To hurry his departure, she moved past him and began walking back up the rise toward their parked vehicles. 'Thanks for stopping by, Mr Bourke. I appreciate your concern.' Her facetious quip told him she did nothing of the sort.

'Ethan.'

In giant strides, he caught up with her, one of his long steps making two of hers. The size of the man beside her was disturbing and comforting at the same time.

'You will be careful, won't you? We're coming into summer. Snake season,' he explained.

She humoured him. 'We do have snakes up north, too.'

They reached their cars, the difference between them profound and incongruous. Ethan's darkly gleaming four-wheel drive and her decrepit ancient van. Before she'd left home, a talented artist friend had painted it with bright flowers.

Ethan prowled around Summer's vehicle and kicked a rear wheel with his boot. 'These tyres are nearly bald.'

'I'm aware they need replacing.' There hadn't been time before she left. Or the money.

He continued with his inspection and peered through a window. 'Is it even roadworthy?'

'Probably.' It still drove. Mechanics wasn't one of her strong points. Why couldn't he ask her something she knew so she didn't feel quite so inadequate? Summer cast an affectionate gaze over her transportation. A few years ago, it had been all she could afford. Even working a second summer job in tourist season had only enabled her to buy the most basic vehicle. 'I prefer to think of Blossom as recycled.'

'*Blossom?*' he spluttered.

His grin eased the hard edge from his face and made him look more human and approachable. Summer also found it hard to stay serious.

'She's perfectly reliable.' She tried to sound injured. 'I've just driven her two thousand kilometres. She was slow but she didn't let me down.'

'Remarkable.' He shook his head. 'All the same, have it checked first thing Monday. See Red Miller at the service station in town and tell him I sent you.'

'Why would I do that? Are you the local god?' she quipped to cover her surprise at his show of concern.

David and Eleanor, off marching in protest about some issue or another, had been casual and loving parents but Summer was left to practically raise herself, making her independent at a very early age. Billy, the man she had foolishly loved, had deserted her before Ivy was born, so she had learned to cope alone.

Her frankness seemed to shock him and his gaze lay on her heavily for a long moment. 'Red's slow but thorough. You can trust him. I'd offer to do it myself but I'm finishing up shearing.'

He would? Summer was surprised by his offer, especially after his initial hostility. 'I wouldn't expect you to.'

He backed away and made to leave. Something changed his mind because he hesitated and turned around to face her. 'By the way, you should get that rusty front gate fixed as soon as possible.'

'Why? I don't plan to close it.'

'It'd be wise if you did. Even these

days, we still get the occasional drover coming through. If you plan on running this farm as a business, I suggest you start thinking that way.'

His censure was deflating. She would have asked him a question about livestock but his arrogance discouraged her.

'Well, welcome to Wombat Creek,' he murmured, like an afterthought.

Summer managed a lukewarm smile at the unexpected sentiment especially since he had done nothing but criticise since he'd arrived.

'Peace,' she mumbled and turned her back on him to slide open the side door of her van, suddenly filled with doubts about her impetuous decision to stay.

Should she reconsider? Could she manage alone? If her grandfather struggled, what made her believe she could succeed? The work ahead suddenly seemed daunting — and expensive. She needed to watch every cent she had squirreled away in recent years while raising Ivy and working two jobs.

From the corner of her eye, as she

gathered up an armful of cardboard boxes, Summer was aware that Ethan had moved away. Moments later, his impressive vehicle purred into life and he drove off down the lane toward the gate. Her gate. Rusted and sagging on its hinges, as he had so carefully pointed out.

She was undecided if she liked him. Considering Ethan Bourke as a friend might prove a challenge.

2

With a long sigh of resignation and laden with gear, Summer trudged over the rampant grass toward the quaint pisé cottage. She stopped to admire her new home, already sensing an uncanny connection. The building's warm ochre walls glowed in the sun, and its sturdy character and rustic charm called to her. Her previous sense of apprehension and intrusion about going inside slowly abated and curiosity took its place.

She would stay, as planned, and she would find her animals, as planned. For Ivy. Even now, if she ignored how much work and time it would take to get there, she could see the grass mowed and her daughter playing in the garden.

She had nothing to prove to him, but she was willing to bet she would show Ethan Bourke that she could make a go of it here.

Because her arms were full to aching, Summer butted open the garden gate with her hip. As she struggled down the brick pathway, she frowned over the rusted roof iron, knowing she didn't have the funds to repair it, yet somehow she must replace it before next winter.

Two chimneys jutted skyward, one toward the front of the cottage, one at the back. She loved the homey romanticism of open fireplaces, although there had been scant need of one in the subtropics further north where she had always lived.

Glancing aside, Summer's green thumb itched to deal with the overgrowth and weeds. She hoped it wasn't too late to prune the roses. It was a temptation to drop her boxes and plunge her hands into the soil right now, but she restrained herself. Her first priority was to prepare the cottage for Ivy's arrival in a few weeks.

Readjusting her load to one side, Summer pushed the giant old key into the lock and opened the stained glass front door. It groaned as she pushed it ajar and invaded the silence within.

A narrow hall ran through the centre of the house, dim and musty from being closed up for months. To her left, a grandfather clock had stopped on six o'clock. Never having owned a watch, Summer doubted she would bother to rewind it. Two open doors either side led into furnished bedrooms, one of which would have been her grand-father's.

Summer dumped her boxes onto the rug in the centre of the living room, removing her hat to toss it onto a plump tapestry sofa. Streaking her fingers through her long hair, she moved through the rooms to explore, pulling up blinds and opening windows.

The more she saw, the more she liked. The furnishings were well-loved, simple and comfortable. A small office had an old table and orderly book-shelves, its leather armchair crinkled and worn with age and use.

A paradise compared to where she

had lived. Her parents had fully embraced a basic lifestyle, so luxuries like hot running water here would be a treat. With hedonistic guilt, Summer realised she would be living a more fulfilling life for the first time in her life. Her principles of self-sufficiency would remain, but she embraced the idea of subtle changes.

When she had brought in the last of her few boxes, Summer drove the ten minutes into the nearby village of Wombat Creek for a few basic supplies and parked Blossom outside the small general store.

The town was one long main street lined with an avenue of eucalypts and boasting the usual assortment of necessary shops, including a bakery, hairdresser, newsagency, post office, tiny local community hall, and service-station-cum-garage.

As she unloaded her few purchases from her basket at the general store checkout, the auburn-haired teenager greeted her warmly. 'How are you today?'

Summer read her name tag. 'Sally?

Hi there.' The girl listened wide-eyed as she introduced herself, explaining she was new in town and where she would be living. 'I don't suppose you know of any alpaca breeders in the district?' Summer asked.

'Can't say I do. But old Sam Guthrie lives next door to your place. You pass right by his gate on your way home. He's lived in the district all his life, knows everything and everybody. He bred angoras a few years back until his health gave out. You'd probably save yourself a lot of time if you go visit him.'

'I'll call on him tomorrow. Do you have a local farmers' market?'

Sally shook her head. 'You could try the community house, though, across the street. Local women call in for a chat and a cuppa any day of the week. They sell crafts and produce. My mum's in the CWA and they meet there once a month. Ask for Jean Miller.'

'Thanks. I will next time I'm in town.'

That would probably need to be tomorrow if she heeded Ethan Bourke's insistence on roadworthy tyres, but she would need to analyse the state of her dwindling bank balance first.

Summer stowed her supplies in the van. She baulked at having to buy fresh fruit and vegetables and couldn't wait until she was ready to grow her own. A thorough garden investigation in the morning would be her first priority.

Back at the cottage, she unpacked her groceries and lit the row of fat candles along the deep windowsill. Arranging power and telephone reconnection were just two of many items on a long list of things to be done in Hamilton tomorrow.

After building and lighting a fire in the wood stove to warm the chilly kitchen, she sliced off a chunk of fresh bread from the loaf she had just bought, dreaming of the day when she could make her own again, and toasted it over the flames for a cheese sandwich. As she nestled into the comfy sofa and sipped her herbal tea, not for the first time over recent months Summer counted her unbelievable blessing to have inherited her grand-father's small farm.

Since Ivy was born, she had worked toward her dream of becoming independent and leasing a few productive acres of her own. Who knew one hundred of them would be dumped in her lap as a gift?

Acquiring Greenbanks over her father had been an unexpected windfall and embarrassment until David assured her he held no regrets or resentment for his father's decision in leaving his estate to his granddaughter instead of his son.

He had also told her that, given his time over again, he would make the same choices again . . . marrying the woman he loved against his parents' wishes and embracing a more liberal lifestyle; leaving home, never to return, the rift between father and son unmended. He and Eleanor, with baby Summer in tow, had drifted north, eventually settling in a sleepy village nestled in a rainforest valley.

As a result, distant from family,

Summer never knew her grandfather. Worse, at eighteen she had made the mistake of falling in love with Billy, innocently believing him when he claimed to love her.

His speedy departure jolted Summer into reality, forcing her to think deeply about the life she really wanted. In the years since, she had quickly matured. Next time, her love would be given much more cautiously and any man in her life would have to earn her trust.

Forming her own opinions as an adult, Summer knew marriage wasn't about the official piece of paper but the commitment and respect each partner had for the other. All the same, she had seen the greater stability of more traditional family units over her parents' casual partners and the younger step-brothers and sisters those liaisons had produced. Not to mention the added chaos of blended families.

Summer rinsed her dishes in the sink and let them drain before conceding to the pull of a soak in the bath. *Ivy is going to love this*, she thought, as she lolled in the water. The thought drew an ache of separation from deep inside her.

More urgent than electricity was getting the telephone reconnected to keep in touch with her daughter while she got the place ready for her. Summer longed to talk to her again — well, Ivy would babble and she would indulgently listen. She must call her parents tomorrow and let them know she had arrived safely.

★ ★ ★

Early next morning, immediately after breakfast, Summer explored the garden. She eventually managed to open the stiff creaky door of a weatherboard tool shed and peer inside. Cobwebs draped the rafters and corners, and a thick layer of dust covered everything inside, but all the tools appeared well-maintained and usable. Outside she stood with her hands on her hips and surveyed the weeds, rampant in overgrown garden beds and knee-high grass.

Starting with a pair of oversized gardening gloves and secateurs, she pruned the rows of roses lining the pathways. The morning hours quickly disappeared as she pulled weeds, only occasionally taking a rest when she kneeled back and surveyed her work just to reassure herself she was actually making progress.

Shielded from the sun by her favourite floppy black felt hat, she revelled in its warmth on her back and arms, losing herself and all sense of time in an effort to start bringing the garden back to life, pleased to notice that the friable soil crumbled easily through her gloved fingers and was in excellent condition.

Mid morning, she took a break, made a pot of herbal tea and took her steaming mug outdoors again to explore further afield in the garden.

Glancing up into the branches of the trees in the rambling orchard to investigate the peaches, apricots and citrus fruits, she heard the faintest mewing. Following the noise to its source, she found a skinny tortoiseshell kitten stranded in the middle branches of an orange tree, looking nervous and adorable. There were no lower branches to gain a foothold and climb up, so she returned to the garden shed for a ladder and rested it against the knotty trunk.

'How did you get up here, and where do you belong?' she crooned, as she edged closer and reached out to rescue the tiny furry bundle — but not without a tussle first.

'That wasn't so bad, was it?' she murmured, cuddling the animal as she descended. 'I'll have you cleaned and fattened up in no time.'

Gardening took second place for a while as she gave the kitten a saucer of milk and watched it hungrily lap it all up. Then she sat in a cane chair on the front porch that looked down across the farm paddocks to the creek, the kitten cradled in her lap on her skirt as she gently picked burrs and leaves from its fur and stroked the nervous animal until it purred, its eyes half closed in contentment.

'You're such a soft colour, I'll have to call you Misty. You've no collar, so if we don't find your owner you can be a wonderful playmate for Ivy.'

After lunch, Summer drove into Wombat Creek. She easily found the garage since it was the only one in the main street and its burly red-haired owner ambled out as she emerged from her van.

'Afternoon. What can I do for you, young lady?'

Summer introduced herself and explained her purpose, shaking his extended hand.

'So you're Amos Dalton's granddaughter, eh? Heard you were in town. We wondered what was going to happen to the old place.' He slowly nodded his head and studied her for a moment. 'Can see the resemblance.' Then he shook his head, wiping his hands on an oily rag as he slowly walked around her vehicle. 'Needs some attention.'

Summer appreciated his tactful understatement. 'Just do what you can but, I have to warn you, I'm on a very tight budget.'

He nodded, understanding. 'Sure. Looks like I'll need to do a roadworthy. I can fix it today. Don't have a customer vehicle but you can borrow my town runabout.' He indicated a small, red, two-door vehicle parked at the side of the garage. 'Sorry it's not more glamorous,' he grinned. 'But I need my better service utility in case I'm called out.'

'You've seen my van. I'm not used to glamorous.'

Red chuckled. 'Reckon you're right about that.'

'I'm heading into Hamilton for a few hours. I'll call by and see how you're going when I get back.' She handed over her keys.

'If I'm not done, you can keep the car overnight.'

Waving goodbye to Red and curling herself into the smaller vehicle, Summer headed toward the main regional town of Hamilton.

Besides the sheep on clover and natural pastures for which the area was renowned, she also noticed beef, dairy cattle and fat lambs grazing in the lush paddocks of the fertile plains.

The rugged sandstone ridges of the Grampian mountains loomed in the north. She knew she was probably less than an hour's drive from the coast to the south. When she was more settled and Ivy was with her again, they could make day trips to the beach.

In the neat, bustling town of Hamilton, with its large stores and supermarkets, she easily located the legal offices of Ryan & Stokes. Although the building exterior was historic and rather grand, the interior had been renovated into a modern office with polished timber floors, smartly dressed young office girls and banks of computers. Broad corridors led away to lawyers' chambers.

With quiet efficiency, Summer was greeted by the same elderly partner again, Mr Stokes, dapper in a pin-striped suit and modest tie, and whisked away to one of the huge old rooms beyond. Because she had called in unexpectedly and late on the day of her arrival, he now had more time to explain the current status of her grandfather's estate and that the process of obtaining probate was well underway.

Summer signed land transfer documents he had now drawn up and finalised before she learned that it would take several months before probate was granted, Greenbanks officially transferred into her name and attendant funds released.

Feeling light-hearted and far more positive about her future with the security of not only a farm but a small reserve of funds, Summer once more silently blessed her grandfather, wondering what karmic instinct had prompted him to choose her as his heir over her father.

When she left the lawyers' offices, she noticed a Telstra office across the street where she arranged reconnection of the telephone out at the cottage. Undeterred that country wheels turned slowly and this might take several days, she focused on spreading her good news. She found a public telephone box on a corner in Grey Street, one of the main roads in town, to call her mother and talk to Ivy. With limited coins and time, she waited with impatient eagerness while they answered.

'Hi, Eleanor.' She launched into a hurried gush of explanations to her mother about the property and district, a high note of enthusiasm in her voice. Usually more quiet than impassioned, it wasn't necessary to mention she planned to stay — Eleanor guessed.

With the essentials covered, Summer asked, 'Is Ivy there?'

'She was playing out on the veranda, but Skye's just brought her in. Here she is now.'

Summer heard muffled voices as the telephone was handed over.

'Mummy?'

Summer almost wept with joy at the sound of her daughter's tiny voice. 'Hey, sweetie. Are you being good for Eleanor?' Her mother refused to be called a grandmother. 'What are you doing today?'

The child launched into a long list of activities, starting with the muesli and yoghurt she had for breakfast, then helping Eleanor in the kitchen and playing with Skye. 'Where are you, Mummy?' she ended wistfully.

'I'm at our new house, darling, making it all clean and right for you when you come down.'

'I miss you, Mummy,' Ivy said plaintively.

'I know, sweetie. I miss you, too, but we have a few more sleeps until I can come and get you.'

'How many sleeps?'

'I don't know, sweetie, but I'll be back as soon as I can.'

After a pause, Ivy's small voice said, 'Okay.'

Summer struggled not to surrender

to a heavy fit of the blues at being separated from Ivy for the first time in her life and questioned whether she should have left the tiny soul so far away.

'When I feel sad in the night, I sleep in Skye's bed.'

Skye was David's next oldest daughter and, by mutual agreement, had always lived with them although her natural mother lived elsewhere. The half-sisters would miss each other when they parted.

'Is David in the house, sweetie?'

'No. He's picking mangoes.'

Summer knew that meant he was in the orchard, a distance from the house, and was disappointed not to speak with him this time.

Because her coins were spent, she said a reluctant but hasty goodbye and hung up. She stared at the telephone handset for a long time before she left the booth and returned to the car, deciding next time she would buy an easier phone card instead.

Before the end of the conversation, Summer had arranged with her mother to call at regular times and talk to Ivy. But for now, armed with punnets of vegetable and herb seedlings she could ill-afford from a hardware store, Summer finally headed back to Wombat Creek, animated at the nippy speed and comfort of her small borrowed car compared to her heavy, chugging van.

At the garage, Summer found Red still balancing the new tyres and giving her battered old vehicle a final check.

'While you wait, why don't you visit the community centre down the street?' he suggested. 'My wife Jean is there with some other women. You could have a cuppa and a chat. Shouldn't be more than an hour.'

'Okay.' Summer agreed and sauntered off along the quiet main street in the direction Red had indicated. It would be an opportunity to meet new people and a chance to make friends. She smiled and greeted the few people she met along the way.

On arrival in the white weatherboard building, she poked her head around the door and swept a quick gaze about the large main room. A plump older woman quietly stitched a quilt in a far corner. A young woman worked at a pottery wheel while two preschoolers played in the toy corner surrounded by a safety fence. The older boy was about Ivy's age and the girl, a toddler, was just walking.

A cheerful, grey-haired woman stepped forward. 'Afternoon, dear.' After studying her for a moment, she beamed and said, 'If I'm not mistaken, you're Amos Dalton's granddaughter. Summer, Sally said. I'm Jean Miller. Sally's my daughter and you've also met my husband, Red, down at the garage. How's your car coming, then?'

Summer smiled. No secrets in this town, then. 'It'll be about an hour.'

'Myrtle, boil the jug.' The lady diligently plying a needle through the quilt set her work aside and rose from her chair. 'Summer, this is Myrtle

Pearce. Best needleworker in the district.'

Myrtle smiled and blushed. 'Just doing what I love.'

Jean nodded sagely. 'Makes all the difference. And Julie over there is married to Lonnie Williams. They run a thousand sheep just out of town. Well, who doesn't around here?' She shrugged, laughing. 'She has a kiln on the farm but when she wants company she comes into town and works here. Leaves her gear set up.'

Summer smiled toward the young woman at the other end of the room and took the seat Jean offered at a central table where, judging by the folder of papers spread out, it looked as if she was organising something.

'Telephone tree for the annual fête.' Jean explained, noticing Summer's glance. 'Our phone bill doubles this time each year checking with all the CWA ladies what craft and cake and jam donations are ready and making arrangements for duty rosters for the tent on the day.

'But that's enough about us.' She laid a hand gently on Summer's arm. 'We were real sad to lose our dear old Amos. Lived in the district all his life. Such a pity David couldn't come back for the funeral.'

There was no malice behind Jean's statement but Summer felt compelled for a second time to explain her father's absence. 'I totally agree, but apparently it was a stipulation in his will.'

Jean's eyes widened. 'Well, I never.' She clicked her tongue and shook her head sadly. 'Amos was a staunch supporter of our little community but he could be a stubborn old beggar. Such a pity when families aren't close, I always say. How are your parents, then?'

'Both well and young at heart. Both have children from other partners so we're rather a blended family.' She paused for a moment giving Jean and all the other listening ears in the room time to digest the information.

When they didn't appear unduly shocked, she continued, 'I have five half-brothers and sisters but I doubt my grandfather knew about them because he and David were never in touch. They let him know when I was born, though. He might have thought I was his only grandchild and that's why he left Greenbanks to me. I was shocked when the letter from the Hamilton lawyers arrived telling me I had inherited the property instead of my father.'

'David must have been hurt over that.'

Summer thought about it for a moment, recalling the discussion she'd had with her father at the time. 'No, I think he was more disappointed that they'd never made amends. Perhaps Amos thought if David walked out on his life and inheritance on the farm, then he didn't deserve it.' Summer shrugged. 'We'll never know, but his resentment must have run deep even after all these years to make that decision.'

At that moment, the clattering of crockery signalled Myrtle's appearance with a pot of tea and cups and saucers on a tray. It was strong and not herbal, but Summer drank it. All the women stopped work, Julie washed her clay-caked hands and they all gathered around the table. The children were given a home-made iced biscuit each but continued playing together in their toy-filled enclosure.

'Is the community centre open every day?'

Jean nodded as she sipped her tea. 'People come and go as they please. Some come just for the company, a chat and a cuppa. Others come to work. Keeps us all in touch and we watch out for each other.'

'Sounds like where I come from.' Summer smiled. 'I suppose Red is not your husband's real name?'

Jean chuckled and helped herself to a second biscuit. 'It's Daniel, but with his hair, he wouldn't be named anything else, would he?'

'Do you have other children besides Sally?'

Jean nodded, her face glowing with warmth. 'Two older boys, Sean and Ryan. Both working on district sheep properties. Sal works at the local supermarket, as you know, and she does housework every week at Karingal Park, too.'

'What family do you have, Myrtle?' Summer made an effort to include the other women in the conversation.

'I'm from a family of six. All of them are married except me. I was the youngest and stayed home to look after my parents. They're both gone now, of course. My father always had a grocery shop in town and I worked there until he sold up and retired.'

'All the district quilting ladies had a bee in recent months, each of them making a square, and Myrtle's stitching it all up together as beautifully as she always does,' Jean put in. 'We're hoping it's going to be the prize and main fundraiser for our raffle this year at the fête. Small communities get forgotten and we have to look after ourselves for money for this and that. We can't always rely on the government, can we?'

Summer intended asking about the fête but Jean babbled on about the Landcare Day in a fortnight. 'Saturday afternoon is sacred for sport around here. Tennis and cricket season has started again so planting will start early on the Saturday morning. Most of the helpers play sport. The local ladies help with catering. Just scones and sandwiches for lunch to feed the volunteers.'

'Can I help?' Summer asked.

'You certainly can. Just come along on the day. I'll phone you a few days beforehand as a reminder. We all meet here in front of the community centre and go out in vehicles in convoy. Our local Landcare environment group has been active for nearly twenty years now. It's independent and community-run, but still on the same principles of caring for the land as the national organisation.

'Most farmers these days are working hard to understand and improve the environment on their own properties. They can do a whole farm planning course to draw up a map and have an aerial photo done to look at the bigger picture. See what issues are facing a property and put certain activities and techniques in place to fix any problems. We'll be on the Tarrants' property helping George do a native planting in a paddock he's fenced off for revegetation.'

In recent years, Summer had done some external off-campus study to obtain a Diploma of Agriculture, preparing herself for the day when she had her own land, although she hadn't envisioned it would happen quite so soon. So she was interested to learn how best to maintain her own small farm, knowing that if she looked after it now, it would reap dividends in the future.

'Amos used to help us on Landcare days, too.' Jean's tone turned reflective.

'A great one for sustainable farming, he was. Greenbanks is in good condition. He made sure of that.'

'Yes. I've noticed. When I've finished weeding and replanting, I'm hoping to bring it back to peak production.'

'Sally tells me you're planning on running alpacas. She was right in recommending your neighbour Sam Guthrie. He's been to specialist field days on raising all kinds of animals. He's slowing up, these days, and doesn't run much livestock any more. Keeps to himself a lot. Always been a bit of a loner and never really got on with Amos. Bad blood from their youth, I gather.'

Jean barrelled on, talking about the Country Women's Association meetings and inviting Summer to come along, writing down her phone number for Summer.

'Mind you, I'm not often at home,' Jean chuckled. 'But there's an answering machine. Just leave a message. I don't have one of those mobile phones that everyone carries around with them these days, practically attached to their ear. Sally bought one as soon as she started working and could afford it. She's never off the thing, chatting and texting to all her friends.'

Summer checked the clock on the wall. 'It's been over an hour since I left the garage. I should go and check if my van's ready.'

'I'll call Red and ask if you like,' Julie offered, swiftly producing a mobile from her bag and making the call. After a brief exchange of conversation, she nodded and gave Summer a thumbs-up sign. 'Still okay if I bring in the four-wheel drive next Tuesday, Red, for a service while I do my shopping? Great. Thanks.' She rose. 'Damon, Jessica, time to go,' she called out to the children in the play enclosure. 'Well, I better be off and get my two into a bath.'

'How old is Damon?' Summer asked.

'Almost four. He starts kindergarten next year.'

'I have a daughter, Ivy, the same age. She's not with me at the moment but I'll be returning up north in a few weeks to get her and bring her back to live with me.'

'Great,' Julie said enthusiastically. 'We need to keep the numbers up with children in the district so the primary school stays open. Every child helps.' she grinned. 'Are you married?'

'No. Single mother. Ivy's father left before she was born.'

'Well, you'll have all the support you need around here. If you run into problems, just ask. Sally Miller's pretty much the resident babysitter around here. She loves kids.'

Julie gathered up her brood, waved and left. Myrtle cleared away the dishes and disappeared into the kitchen again.

Jean sighed and struggled to her feet. 'Well I better go home and make these phone calls and organise something for dinner. Glad you stopped by, Summer. Feel free to do so any day, including weekends. It was lovely to meet you.'

3

On the drive home, after collecting her
van from the garage, Summer noted
how much better it was running since
Red's attention. Although he had generously charged her only cost price for the
new tyres, he'd said the vehicle had long
since seen better days and he couldn't
guarantee that Blossom wouldn't one
day let her down on the road somewhere. He hadn't told her something
she didn't already know, but the old
clunker had been a part of her life,
almost like family, for years now and
she would find it difficult to part with it.

Before reaching Greenbanks, Summer
slowed and, on a whim, turned in at
Sam Guthrie's driveway to introduce
herself and seek his advice.

The short, tree-lined driveway of
ancient scrappy pines led to a rambling,
older, red-bricked house with an untidy

garden. She pulled up in the open gravelled area alongside the house and found her way around to the back door. She knocked and called out through the screen door. 'Hello. Anyone home?'

As the wiry balding gentleman shuffled into sight, he abruptly halted and gaped. Understandable, thought Summer, since she was the image of her father, and he probably noticed the resemblance. He stared at her, vacant and distant, for a long while.

Eventually, appearing visibly shaken and disoriented, he croaked uncertainly, 'Catherine?'

Sam didn't seem to emerge from his confusion until Summer answered, 'No, I'm Summer Dalton, Amos' grand-daughter. Were you expecting someone else?'

His face cleared and his gaze focused. 'Ah. Of course. You look so much like . . . ' He paused.

'My father?'

'No.' He frowned. 'Like your grand-mother, Catherine.'

Summer's interest sharpened. Her grandmother. Sam was of a similar age and would have known her. Perhaps this or subsequent visits might be a chance to learn more about the grandparents she never knew. If he was prepared to talk about them, that is. Jean had made some comment earlier this afternoon about bad blood between them, leaving Summer to wonder what could have happened.

'If you're going to be my new neighbour you'd better come in, then.'

Not the warmest welcome she had ever received but Summer accepted his indifferent offer with a smile and stepped into the huge country kitchen, untidy with dishes in the sink and newspapers, some in a pile and another half-open, on the table.

He pulled out a chair. 'Sit yourself down.' He trudged over to a dated Hecla electric jug and set it to boil. She'd seen such collectible items for sale in second-hand shops, and was surprised and not a little alarmed to see it still working.

She grinned to herself at the thought of yet another sociable cup of tea for the afternoon but would never have refused. Over the noise of the water thundering to a boil, Summer said, 'I guess it must have been a shock for you to see me?'

'Don't get many visitors,' he muttered.

Any wonder with his grumpy manner, Summer thought and filed away the information that he'd avoided directly answering her question.

She decided to test his reaction and gently led into the subject of her family. 'My father never returned here, and we had no contact with our grandfather.' With no answer, she continued as though speaking to herself. 'Makes me wonder if Amos ever mentioned us.'

She needed to know if his estranged family was ever in her grandfather's thoughts. He must have given them some consideration because he had made her his heir.

'Can't say as he did,' Sam replied

with his back to her. 'The Daltons and the Guthries kept their distance.'

And yet they had lived only a few miles apart. Jean's claim had been right. 'Really?' Summer tried to sound surprised to cover her disappointment. 'That would have been unusual, living in the country where neighbours need to rely on each other.'

Sam turned off the madly boiling non-automatic jug and poured water into a teapot, then covered it with a knitted cosy. A charming old-fashioned habit few people performed these days since the invention of the tea bag. But Sam hailed from another generation where the practice would have been commonplace.

When he turned around, he gave her another long concentrated stare before setting the teapot, a sugar bowl, a packet of shortbread biscuits and a small carton of milk on the table. Seated opposite and leaving the tea to steep with only the ticking of the kitchen clock in the background, he then went through the process of filling and lighting up a pipe.

Taking in the scowl of concentration across his weathered forehead, Summer decided silence was wise and patiently waited, for she was certain he wanted to say more. Her democratic upbringing had taught her to listen and learn before any evaluation. Since childhood, she'd been a welcome part of the regular, open and friendly community meetings usually held sitting in a circle under a tree.

After he took the first puffs and smoke rose in a thick cloud toward the kitchen ceiling, Sam cleared his throat and said quietly, 'No Dalton has crossed my doorstep for over forty years.' He looked past her absently for a moment. 'Since Amos was your grandfather, mebbe you have a right to know . . . ' There was a long pause before he added simply, 'He married the woman I loved.'

The weight of perhaps never taking anyone else into his confidence, and the passage of many years in between, brought a touching sadness to his softly uttered words; a confession it was obvious he had been reluctant to make.

From an early age, Summer had been attuned to people's feelings. Her heart went out to him to see the agony of memory on his face and she reached out a slender brown hand across the table to cover his, blotched and wrinkled with age.

She took the initiative and poured their tea, by now brewed as strong as syrup. 'I'm sorry to hear that. Do you want to talk about it?' she dared to ask. She hoped that, if he was willing, the process of dealing with his past might prove therapeutic and begin the healing process to bring the Daltons and Guthries once more together in neighbourly friendship.

To her relief and pleasure, Sam Guthrie began to reminisce.

'I loved Catherine from the time we first went to school together. She was the loveliest fragile thing. Hair black as the darkest night.'

His gaze drifted toward Summer and he gave a gentle sigh. 'So much like yours and just as long. Incredible.' He shook his head, staring at her again before breaking his gaze. 'In those days it was always in two braids but as she grew older, she swept it up into a pile at the back of her head. As we grew up, I couldn't wait to get to dances and hold her in my arms. I imagined that I would protect her for life. I called on her most Sundays and we often stepped out together socially.'

Sam drew on his pipe again and his brows dipped low together in a habit Summer was beginning to recognise foretold another bout of grumps. 'But then, almost overnight, Amos-bloody-Dalton caught her attention. She'd never given him a second glance before. But he pressed his advantage — and won.'

Summer winced. 'Unreturned love hurts.' As well she knew for herself from Billy's rejection.

'I know it was fate. You can't force

someone to love you for real. When it's returned, I imagine it's rather special. To have the other person care as much as you do. But I just couldn't move on and hated seeing her so happy with someone else. I never married, just in case she was ever widowed or needed me. I wanted to be available for her. Always.'

He glanced across at Summer, emerging from his trance-like recollections. 'I have a photograph of her, of Catherine. She gave it to me just before she became engaged to Amos. Even though she loved him, she still thought of me. That was the woman I fell in love with. Would you like to see it?' he asked, already rising.

Summer nodded. 'Absolutely. I've never seen her picture.'

She didn't add that she would likely find one in the cottage when she could bear to invade what felt like her grandfather's privacy and go through cupboards and drawers; it was too soon for her to do that. As much as she felt attuned

61

to her new home, she needed to feel a deeper sense of belonging, and she knew that would only come with time.

As she heard Sam rustling about down the passage in another room, she decided, whether he liked it or not, she was going to become a good neighbour for the lonely old bachelor — even at the risk of making a nuisance of herself.

His love for her grandmother had been genuine and profound, for he had forsaken all others. Not usually romantic — and deceived, the one time she had fallen in love with irresponsible, selfish Billy — Summer could only hope she found such a lasting love one day, too.

When Sam returned with Catherine's photograph, he laid the large cardboard-framed studio portrait reverently on the table in front of her as though the subject was a saint — and to Sam, she probably was.

Summer gasped. 'You're right — I am like her!'

Catherine Dalton was a younger mirror image of herself and she finally understood Sam's shock at the sight of her when she had arrived, especially in the light of his emotional confidences and confessions just now. Seen from inside the house with the daylight behind her, his memory and eyesight had clearly played tricks and, with the uncertainty of age, he had been easily mistaken.

The beautiful young woman with up-swept hair, exactly as Sam had described, stood serenely beside a pedestal of flowers and in front of a false painted window backdrop.

'I've seen a photograph of Amos when he was younger, but never my grandmother. Thank you for sharing her with me. It means a lot.'

'Me too, girlie, me too.'

There wasn't a smile on his face but there wasn't a scowl either, so Summer could only hope that meant a positive sign for the future.

'It's handy that you're my neighbour

because Jean Miller suggested I come and see you,' she ventured.

'Wretched woman sticks her nose into everything. Why would she do that?' he said, grumpy again.

Uh-oh, she'd spoken too soon. But she ignored his surliness, knowing the deeper character of the man now, suspecting it was only a cover to alienate people and not let them into his heart against the possibility of being so badly hurt again.

'Because I want to breed alpacas on Greenbanks,' she explained. 'And I'm told you're the guru of information about them.'

'Alpacas.' Sam rubbed his chin. 'Well, I'll be darned. Why would you want to do that?'

'Mainly as a backup income but many others reasons as well. I've been doing some research.' She began ticking them off on her fingers. 'They're easy keepers, eat small amounts of hay, do well on small acreage, have a gentle disposition, and I understand there's a growing demand for fine quality fleece. I've heard there's not enough to satisfy local demand, let alone the international market.'

'I'm impressed.' Was that a sparkle in his old grey eyes?

'And they're designer green,' she announced proudly. 'Their soft padded feet are gentle on the soil, they're more efficient and don't graze low like sheep and they do well on native grasses as well as pasture.'

Sam remained quiet awhile, thinking and rubbing his chin. 'You'd only need to mebbe buy two or three animals initially, preferably ones that are used to being touched and haltered. Eventually you could stock four or five an acre. Average herd is probably about twenty animals. A weanling female will be cheaper than one of breeding age. Pregnant females are more and the price depends on the stud.' Livening up, he added, 'You'd need a regular source of hay, of course, and a feed supplement over the winter. It'll take time to build your herd,' he warned. 'They're slow breeders. Only one off-spring each year.'

'How do you know so much?' Summer asked in admiration.

The corners of his eyes crinkled and an edge of humour touched his lips. 'Been around a while, girlie. Keep my eyes and ears open.'

When he let down his guard to reveal a softer side, Summer recognised he could become not only a valuable friend but a wonderful surrogate grandfather for Ivy.

Sam turned thoughtful, then told her about weekend alpaca workshops held locally on a stud property down near the coast. 'On the Peters' place. They go in for 'em in a big way.' He shuffled about, found a small notepad and pen to write down the details.

Later, after disappearing off some-where in the house again, he produced some farming magazines for her to read on the subject. 'Be your best bet for buying in stock to start your breeding programme. Unless you're going in for fleece.'

'Fleece will be a consideration for my own spinning but, long-term, I plan to breed them.'

'Well, be warned,' Sam said. Summer prepared herself for some gloomy statistics or ominous predictions. 'Alpacas are adorable.'

She laughed and shook her head. 'You keep that sense of humour of yours well hidden, Sam Guthrie. By the way,' she added on an idle thought, 'You don't also know where I can buy chooks, do you? Amos has poultry yards set up and I'd like to make use of them.'

'Well now.' Sam readjusted his battered hat and rubbed his chin. 'I'm gettin' too old to be lookin' after too many animals any more. You're welcome to the youngest and best of my layers if you want.'

Sam's offer blew her away and the crusty old bloke wasn't just being nice, he was serious and genuine.

Within twenty minutes they had

inspected and chosen five hens, depleting his stock by half, which he claimed he was more than happy to do. With surprising agility for his age, he caught and caged them for easy transportation to take home, refusing payment but gingerly suggesting a trading arrangement of future produce from Summer's fruit and vegetable yields, to which she readily agreed — but not before she gave in to a quick hug of warmth for his kindness.

Embarrassed by her impulsive action, he looked away and said gruffly, 'Ought to get those roof leaks of yours fixed before summer thunderstorms. Can sweep in sudden and dump an inch of rain.'

'I know,' she groaned with humour. 'It's one of a long list of catch-up jobs I need to do yesterday.' Summer considered his previous comment and frowned in confusion. 'How do you know anything about the cottage if you never visit?'

Sam nodded toward the road. 'Him.'

As they lingered in the yard beside

her van with the chooks clucking in their cages inside, Ethan Bourke's shiny big vehicle drove past. With an elbow resting on the open window, he glanced in their direction and raised his arm in a leisurely wave.

Sam squinted at her from under his hat. 'Know your other neighbour?'

Summer nodded. 'We've met.'

'He's still a bachelor. A good catch but comes with family baggage. Don't reckon he knows it himself.'

She raised interested eyebrows but didn't press him to elaborate. 'I hate to push our friendship, Sam, because you've been so generous already but I don't suppose you have a trailer I could borrow to bring home any animals I buy?'

'Sure do.' His eyes twinkled with animation. 'I could come down and help you, too, if you like.'

Summer didn't have the heart to refuse his kindness; he would probably enjoy the outing and she was only too happy to oblige.

'It's a date.' She smiled.

As Summer drove home later, she couldn't help being intrigued by Sam's remark about Ethan Bourke's problem. She wouldn't have thought he was a man to have any.

4

By the time she returned to Greenbanks and contended with the squawking release of her new arrivals into the poultry run, Summer had forgotten all about her puzzling neighbour. Trying to calm the hens, she talked to them, as she instinctively did to all animals, as they flapped to freedom in the yard.

Doing what her parents had always done with their poultry, she named them. 'Anastasia, Dominica, Isabella, Esmeralda . . . and you will be Henrietta.' She chuckled at the irony of the most appropriate name as she released the last one. 'Ivy is going to love chasing you all around.'

Once feathers stopped flying and they were happily pecking at the pellets she had poured into their feeding bin, she laid fresh straw into the egg-laying boxes, brought from bales in the bigger farm shed on the property, then decided to use the remaining daylight hours to make a further attack on the garden.

She weeded, hoed and spread manure on the existing kitchen garden beds then nestled the thyme, basil and oregano seedlings she had bought in Hamilton into the soil to complement the basic parsley, mint and rosemary already planted, keeping aside one plant of each for pots on the kitchen windowsill.

★ ★ ★

Next morning, as she scattered leafy kitchen scraps around the yard for her scratching hens, Summer heard a vehicle approach, heralded by a thin cloud of dust. She was learning to recognise the sounds that drifted to her outdoors on the wind. When her neighbour appeared, she was pleased with herself for guessing right.

'You're impossible to contact. You have no landline or mobile,' came Ethan's blunt greeting accompanied by a scowl as he strode toward her.

'Maybe I like it that way,' she said with a playful smile, leading him on since she had already arranged to have it reconnected — although not holding her breath as to when it might actually happen.

'Out here, a woman alone, you should give it priority.'

'I'm not concerned. Everyone I've met so far has been nothing but friendly. Besides, I can't do everything at once,' she pointed out calmly.

'It's a damn nuisance, chasing over here every time I want to talk to you,' he continued.

'Then don't.' She paused. 'Why did you come, anyway?'

'I have a proposition for you . . . inside?' He stepped away from her.

'Careful. Esmeralda's behind you.'

A rush of beating wings made him stop and look down. 'You're kidding. Sam's?' Summer nodded. 'I was surprised to see him speaking to you yesterday, what with you being a relation of Amos.'

'He's a very lonely old man clinging to the past. We did just fine. Come up to the house and I'll make you a cold drink.'

She didn't miss Ethan's genuine expression of surprise at her friendship with Sam, nor his obvious admiration as his sharp sweeping gaze from beneath his low-tugged Akubra took in her work in the garden and around the house since his visit the first day she arrived.

'You've put in a lot of hours already,' he reluctantly acknowledged.

Summer glowed with personal pride. High praise from a man she suspected was disinclined to give it.

She'd spent the last two days hacking the garden into better shape, endlessly weeding and mulching ready for the warm summer days ahead, gratified with her efforts and rewarded with the dampness of evening watering to see new shoots appearing on trimmed shrubs and fresh greenery everywhere. At this rate, she would be able to bring

Ivy down sooner than she planned.

'Mind your head,' she warned as she ducked beneath a row of wind chimes tinkling in the morning breeze along the front porch.

The moment she stepped over her threshold, the smell of baking wafted into her senses from the vegetable muffins she had taken out of the oven after breakfast.

'I have fresh chilled lemonade, or would you prefer herbal tea?'

'Neither, actually. I'm here on business,' he added briskly, looking slightly uncomfortable.

Oh, dear. Privately amused, Summer braced herself for whatever suggestion he had in mind. 'Surely you have time for a drink.'

She poured him a cold glass and set it on the table in front of him, gesturing that he take a seat.

He seemed uneasy and watchful at her hospitality, especially since she guessed the matter for discussion appeared serious or unpleasant.

His interested gaze had roamed around the cottage rooms as they had walked through. He would notice changes. If he ran true to form he probably wouldn't approve, but it was her home now and she had begun to put her own personal touches into it — large cushions on the floor where she sat most of the time; her spinning wheel biding time in a corner of the living area with skeins of mohair she'd not yet had a chance to make up . . . perhaps in the autumn. Misty scampered into the room from somewhere else in the house.

'Where did he come from?' Ethan asked.

'It's a she, actually. Stuck up a tree in the orchard. I don't suppose you recognise her, do you? She seemed neglected and most definitely lost.'

Ethan shook his head. 'Could have wandered miles.'

She set the plate of warm muffins on the table and was surprised when he took one. Pouring herself a glass of iced water and seating herself opposite her visitor, Summer's patience paid off when Ethan finished a mouthful of cake, took a deep gulp of his drink, then finally broached the subject on his mind.

'Do you believe you can successfully farm this property?'

The inference in his overbearing tone told her he had already decided that she could not. She wondered where the loaded question was leading. She wasn't offended, more disappointed in his lack of faith and confidence in her.

'Who said anything about being a raging success? I just want a place to live that will return me a living. I know I can make Greenbanks productive enough for my needs.'

'An admirable philosophy, but in this country it seems a waste of valuable land. Do you realise you're sitting on a gold mine?'

Taken aback by his blatant financial consideration above all else, she said, 'No, I'm sitting on a family farm. One that I was extremely fortunate to have passed on to me in trust, to take care of during my lifetime and for my own children one day.'

He shrugged. 'There are big dollars being paid for properties in the district. Tens of thousands an acre. You work it out.'

'I don't need to. I'm not selling.' She'd given absolutely no thought to doing so and felt confronted by his suggestion.

'This district is all bought up and settled. Land is in demand.' He paused. Giving her time to do the calculations, she wondered? 'Name your price. I'd be prepared to buy you out.'

She gaped, incredulous. 'You're serious, aren't you?'

She studied him for a moment, seated so autocratically at her scrubbed kitchen table, not sure whether he realised he had offended her by suggesting she couldn't make a go of it here or that she should bail out before she had even tried. 'How many acres is Karingal Park?'

'Five thousand,' he told her without hesitation.

'With such a substantial property already, why would you want my insignificant one hundred acres?'

'Just thought it might be an option for you,' he said.

'To save face before I fall flat on it?' Summer teased with a chuckle.

He named a figure and Summer spluttered the sip of water she had just taken. 'That's obscene.'

'The amount or the offer?'

'Both. It doesn't matter how high you go, I'm staying.'

'Well, when you change your mind — '

'I won't,' Summer interrupted. It took a lifetime of practised composure to stay calm.

'My offer still stands.'

'So does my refusal.'

The tension in the kitchen between them across the table was substantial, so it was some time before either of them spoke again. Summer because she dared not and Ethan, she supposed, because he was in shock, having expected her to jump at his offer.

Finally, he rose and said with a surprising amount of concern, 'I hope you're not making a mistake.'

She shrugged a slim shoulder. 'Time will tell, won't it?'

He hesitated, circling his hat in his hands. 'I'll let myself out.'

After he left, Summer sat cross-legged on the cushion in the middle of the living room floor, spread her hands gently over her knees and closed her eyes. A spot of disciplined meditation usually worked when she was tense, but this morning her thoughts kept bouncing back to all the people she had met in the town and her farming neighbours.

From their first meeting, Ethan Bourke had left the greatest impression. You could overlook his forceful personality once you became used to his bossy ways. The upside was that innate strength and feeling of absolute protection that oozed from every pore of his very handsome body. No woman alive could help but notice.

Summer's judgments of people usually stood her well but, on reflection, she questioned if her instincts had let her down this time. She found the quandary unsettling.

She'd always nursed the hope that, despite Bourke's natural sense of self-importance, she might be able to chisel through his reserve so they could become friends. But having experienced yet another blast of his condescension, she harboured doubts. It left her feeling a deep sense of loss, but for what exactly, she didn't know.

She could only conclude that Ethan Bourke either didn't want her in the district or considered her a fleeting resident not destined to prosper. Shades of chauvinism or prejudice? Only time would prove to such a sceptic that she was not only a stayer with long term goals, but would make Greenbanks a productive property and permanent family home.

Every day for the rest of the week Summer laboured with love in the garden and cleared scrappy pockets of untidiness around the cottage, pruning the lavender back hard and the avenues of roses along pathways, as well as waging a continual battle with weeds, gratified to note she was gaining.

After breakfast, and dressing in her basic gardening garb of striped cotton trousers and a floppy shirt, she kneaded dough for another loaf of her favourite rye bread, then prepared and left a casserole and pot of soup to simmer on the stove, allowing her the freedom and luxury to lose track of time outdoors.

Every time she passed the rosemary, she trailed her fingers along a branch and inhaled its stimulating scent on her hands. She grew browner and fitter, inspired by the results of tiny claret shoots on the roses and flourishing healthy plants responding to her attention. Misty became her playful shadow, pouncing around her in the garden, snooping curiously and never far away.

Her girls in the chook yard clucked around her ankles when she fed them each day, letting them roam free around the paddock before being penned up again at night. She swore they knew their names now when she talked to them as she crossed the yard to collect the eggs or tossed them handfuls of leafy kitchen scraps.

The power and telephone were reconnected so, technically, there was no longer any need for Summer to use candles but she loved them and invariably lit a few for soft lighting in the evenings.

Regular phone calls to Ivy wrenched her emotions every time she spoke to her daughter back home . . . She must stop thinking of New South Wales as home. Greenbanks took that honour now and she couldn't wait to collect her lively daughter and bring her here to start their new life together. It hadn't been easy, knowing her decision meant taking Ivy away from her grandparents with whom she was close.

Apart from Ethan Bourke's gruffness, she had been readily welcomed into this small district community, so Ivy would soon make new friends and settle down, too. As it had been her parents' prerogative to leave this place, now it was hers, one generation later, to return.

In the evenings, or if the late spring afternoons became too hot for gardening, Summer began spring cleaning the house. She felt invasive opening and sorting the contents of cupboards and shelves and drawers but to her disappointment hadn't discovered many family treasures — not of the material kind, but of memorable or personal value that might have helped her learn more about Amos and Catherine. Either her grandparents had not been sentimental, or they had been masters of recycling long before it was fashionable.

Of the few photographs she found,

there was one glorious wedding photograph of Amos and Catherine; he dapper in a formal suit and she, just as lovely as the picture Sam had shown her, a pearl tiara set amongst her elegant upswept hair and holding a full length veil, the flowing satin dress simple with a sweetheart neckline.

When not indoors, Summer was out spending countless hours tramping over virtually every acre she owned. She discovered sound fencing on the property and the ideal layout of smaller paddocks close to the cottage as most suitable and ready for the alpacas she planned to buy and breed.

Resting her arms on a fence post, she reined in her excitement as she surveyed the pastoral world within her own small kingdom and the lush countryside beyond, knowing that before she bought her first stock, she needed to educate herself about raising them.

Poring over the magazines Sam had lent her, Summer investigated and enrolled in an introductory workshop and training weekend for potential owners. The residential conference retreat that included meals and accommodation was near the coast. She filled with pleasure, realising her objective was one step closer.

Sitting with her feet tucked beneath her on a cushion and eating a lentil and vegetable bake by candlelight, Summer had not long ended the phone call confirming her workshop booking when the telephone shrilled out through the cottage again.

'I haven't seen you in town or at the community centre. Are you okay out there?' She smiled at Jean's motherly concern, having left a message with her new telephone number.

'I've been busy. And I bartered chooks from Sam, in exchange for staples once my garden's producing.'

'That sounds friendly — and most unlike Sam, I have to say,' Jean observed. 'But I'm pleased to hear it. Might mean better things to come for both your families.'

'I hope so.'

'Just a reminder about the Landcare day weekend after next. Are you still able to make scones for lunch?'

'Absolutely.' Summer smiled.

'Good. I'll put you on the roster. Couple of dozen should do it, it's not a big day. We should be done in a few hours.'

'I could make some savoury zucchini muffins as well, if you like?' Summer suggested.

'Sounds too healthy for me,' Jean chuckled. 'But please do. Not everyone's interested in baking these days. Young mums are often working and simply don't have the time. Nice to hear a few still enjoy keeping up the old traditions.'

'It's a love I inherited from my mother, really.'

'With all the lemons and oranges off those trees of yours, you should be able to make loads of marmalade. The first of the apricots and peaches should be bearing in your orchard by Christmas.'

'Yes, the branches are drooping with fruit. So, how many people turn up to the Landcare planting days?'

'Well, me, of course. I organise the women. Usually the same twenty or so. Ethan Bourke co-ordinates it all overall. He organises the men for bringing out any heavy stuff, orders and collects the plants from the wholesale native nursery. He's pretty much hands-on in the community. Don't know where he gets his energy. Seems driven.'

'I imagine if his family were one of the earliest settlers in the district, they've been stalwarts of the community for a long time.'

'Certainly have. Ethan's on the other side of thirty so he's the district's most eligible bachelor. I tell you, he's a natural. He charms women, children and dogs. I would have thought that girlfriend of his, Meredith Wells, would have dragged him to the altar in some big church years ago. But it still hasn't happened. I'll believe it when I see it.'

That was the first time Summer had

heard anyone mention a woman in Ethan's life. 'I didn't realise he had a partner.'

'Oh, she's not really a partner. Meredith lives in Sydney and rarely comes down here to Victoria.'

Summer wondered what kind of relationship that produced. Not one to be taken too seriously, perhaps?

'They grew up together,' Jean went on, 'And I think both their parents expect them to make an announcement one day. One of them would have to make a big sacrifice and move interstate for that to happen, though. Oh, talking of moving, that reminds me . . . ' Jean changed the subject. 'There's an elderly lady in town, Enid Meyer, has lived here all her life but the dear old soul can't look after herself any more so she's moving into The Birches care centre in Hamilton. They don't accept animals, of course, and she has this beautiful young sheltie, Laddie, that needs a good home. Don't suppose you know where we could find one?'

'Have you heard about me adopting Misty and think I'm a soft touch, then?' Summer teased.

'Well now, you do have plenty of space out there, don't you?'

Summer considered the possibility. If the dog was young, it might be easier to settle him as part of another family. Shelties weren't overly big dogs and, from what she knew, were companionable. Although David had never allowed any of his children to have pets so close to protected rainforest, down here on her generous acreage was a different situation.

'Oh, all right, Jean. I'll take him, but if he doesn't work out when Ivy gets here, I'll need to find him another home.'

'Fair enough.' She gave Summer Enid's address, suggesting a few visits so she and the dog could get to know each other.

'I can't take him this weekend. I'll be away at an alpaca workshop near Port Fairy, and I wouldn't want to leave him alone in new surroundings.'

'I'll let Enid know. She's been that worried. It will be such a relief for her. She has no family close by, and so far no one's come forward to look after Laddie. Caring for any animal is a big responsibility, so I appreciate your offer, Summer.'

'I'll call in on my way through to the coast at the weekend and maybe again on the way home, see how the dog and I get on.'

5

Early Saturday morning, roaring down the A200 from Wombat Creek toward the coast in her noisy van, Summer reflected on the visit she had just made. Enid Meyer was a dear old thing, the kind of grandmotherly figure she'd never had in her own life, but at eighty-two, no longer as mobile or able to manage alone. Laddie proved to be well trained from a puppy and, although wary of her at first, became more trusting by the time she left. She'd no doubt they would become friends.

Summer learned that shelties did well with children if they were raised with them from an early age, so she was glad he'd have time to adjust to new surroundings before Ivy arrived.

Reaching the turnoff to the alpaca property, Summer's full attention was soon swept up by large numbers of animals grazing in smaller paddocks as she drove toward the homestead. Signs directed her to the conference buildings at the rear in a lodge separate from the main house.

After meeting her fellow attendees, they started classroom sessions, learning the basics and networking over cuppas and midday lunch. The main area easily converted into a dining room for the evening meal with a quick rearrangement of tables and chairs.

The next day was more hands-on training when they moved outdoors walking between paddocks and sheds for classes, boosting Summer's confidence and knowledge. No question was considered a silly question, particularly reassuring when it came to individual practice in the shearing shed, injections, toenail clipping, and halter training.

Having her first close contact with the beautiful, tractable animals and the bond she quickly established with some of the herd, convinced Summer she was making the right decision. The cordiality of their hosts, Jenny and Ross Peters, ensured they would become her mentors should she ever need support.

She was also delighted to discover that besides owning alpacas for pets or breeding, agistment — taking in others' herds for grazing — was another option, and a quick way for her to create an upfront income.

By late Sunday, when it was time to climb into Blossom and head back to Wombat Creek, Summer had become part of a whole different community of people with a specialist interest, and made more new friends. She left feeling enthused and positive about her future and the direction of her farming decision.

She also cemented her friendship with Laddie with another visit to Enid, who had spent the weekend with helpers in her lovely old family home in a nostalgic clearing-out of a lifetime's accumulated possessions.

But during the week when Summer

returned to take the dog to his new home on the farm, Enid grew distraught as Laddie leaped into the van and her close companion was about to leave. In reassurance, Summer offered to bring the dog back for regular visits to Enid's new home. She even suggested future outings to Greenbanks for a visit, which the elderly lady willingly accepted amid hugs and tears before they drove away.

* * *

Summer rose early for tree-planting the following weekend, baking scones and muffins for lunch. Leaving Misty and Laddie to keep each other company for a few hours, she packed the food into a huge hamper she had found in the hall cupboard and rumbled into Wombat Creek where others had already gathered in front of the community centre.

'Morning.' Jean greeted her in the crisp spring air. Summer was glad she had worn her only pair of jeans. The sudden chill of early morning and a stiff southerly heralded a cool change overnight from the recent spell of warm weather.

She transferred her hamper into the trunk of Jean's station wagon, already loaded with other baskets, paper cups and huge portable urns of hot water before she joined a group quietly chatting, but lost track of the conversation when she looked over someone's shoulder to see Ethan stacking large plastic trays of native seedlings into the back of his Range Rover. As always, he looked good — and impossible to ignore — not at all like the cynic who had implied she was a flop and offered to buy her out.

When it came time to head out in convoy to the planting property, Jean walked over and said kindly, 'We'll be driving over rough terrain, dear. I don't think Blossom's suitable. I'd offer to give you a lift but my car's already full.'

Summer was fully aware of her van's limitations. Looking around for other possibilities for a ride, Ethan glanced in her direction. Catching sight of her for the first time, he raised his eyebrows in surprise. Recovering, he stepped closer. 'I have room for one more. Jump in.'

She groaned silently. Trust his vehicle to be the only one available! And why be so nice to her in public and so mean in private? Still wary, despite how glowingly others always spoke of him, Summer decided she really must be more tolerant.

She hated herself for accepting with a smile. 'Sure. Why not?' She hardly had much of a choice with all the other vehicles full.

Ethan turned aside and spoke to a middle-aged man and two young women, who climbed up into the back, leaving the front seat for Summer. As she greeted the others settling themselves behind her and clicked on her seat belt, her quick gaze took in the polished timber trim and leather seats of the comfortable luxury four-wheel drive.

When Ethan swung into the driver's

seat beside her, the vehicle immediately took on the forceful power of his arresting personality. Wearing his familiar Akubra with worn jeans and a thick black jumper with leather elbow patches, he looked half normal. She might even be tempted to consider him handsome and exciting.

Speeding out of town, the three passengers in the back obviously knew each other and chatted among themselves, leaving Summer and Ethan to make their own conversation.

She decided to leave it up to him. Eventually, he said, 'I was surprised to see you today.'

She pulled a tight smile. 'Why should it be such a stretch to believe that I have respect for nature and the planet the same as you?'

The devilish side of her kept wanting to push him, spark a response, bring out the lighter side buried so deep instead of the serious public image he usually showed to the world, as if he was reluctant to let down his guard and reveal his true self.

After a while he said quietly, 'I guess I don't know you very well.'

'You certainly don't.' She paused. 'And to answer your question, I volunteered like everyone else because I care about the environment and, being new in town, it's a way to meet people.'

'If you plan on staying,' he responded in soft challenge.

She turned away from him to glance out of her window. 'I won't dignify that with an answer.'

'I take it you haven't reconsidered my offer, then?'

'My grandfather believed in me. Why can't you?'

'I'll be watching you with interest.'

Honestly, he was an utterly exasperating man! 'I can send you weekly reports,' she offered, annoyed to feel so drawn to him, even as he criticised her.

After a pause, Ethan said, 'I came over to see you last weekend. You weren't around.'

'No.' She didn't elaborate. Her movements were none of his business.

Silence fell between them again until they turned off the sealed highway and headed down a gravelled track toward low hills with deeply eroded gullies. Ahead, a large paddock was fenced off without stock. Previous young plantings had already taken place with banks of seedlings covering the furthest slopes to stabilise the soil and regenerate the area. Higher up, natural runoff had been redirected with diversion banks and contour cultivation over a number of levels to modify water moving through the gully. With only minor damage so far, the landowner had wisely started early preventative action before any further deterioration occurred.

Because she had already scoured every acre of her own property, Summer knew this problem did not exist at Greenbanks and silently thanked her grandfather for leaving it in premium condition.

A girl from the first of the convoy vehicles opened a farm gate, standing aside while all the cars drove through and pulled up on a flat area at the bottom of a hill. Everyone clambered out. It soon became apparent they had all worked together before because the volunteers immediately gathered tools, digging forks, trays of seedlings and boxes of plastic tree guards. Someone had towed a watering tanker on a small trailer for after planting.

Two of the men helped Jean erect an awning tent without sides and set up lightweight portable tables beneath. Everyone was channelled into groups. As luck would have it, Summer found herself attached to Ethan, probably because she had driven out with him, and assigned the task of laying out the seedling tubes in their allocated area.

The whole process was well organised but, rather than seeming like work, it was apparent from the calling-out and banter among them all that the helpers considered it fun.

The two teenage girls gravitated toward each other, chattering and laughing, clearly friends, throwing Ethan and Summer together. She followed his lead after digging holes and they were soon on their knees, windblown and gloved hands in the soil, planting. Incredibly, a quiet harmony slid into place between them as they worked together.

'I understand you live with your mother?' The casual question tumbled out after Summer adjusted to his company and her resentment eased.

Ethan nodded. 'Uh-huh.'

'She's not an outdoor person, then?'

He flashed her a sharp glance accompanied by a wry grin. Whatever she had said amused him enough to break through his crust and when his mouth gently tilted, she melted in the wake of its charm.

'You haven't met Victoria.' He stopped working and turned thoughtful. 'She pays a fortune for manicured nails,' he revealed quietly. 'I doubt she'd want to jeopardise them.' There was an echo of sadness behind his casual statement.

Picking up on it, Summer filled with compassion. 'How does she like to spend her time, then?'

'Shopping, eating out, playing hostess. She was born and raised on the property but hated it so I've always wondered why she married my father and stayed. Not complaining,' he grinned. 'I got to grow up there.'

'The country has its compensations.' They shared a grin and she endured his steady gaze, recalling the utter joy and freedom of her own childhood in a small hinterland town on the north coast without much parental supervision.

'Most women prefer the city these days.' He frowned.

Summer recalled Jean's words about his girlfriend in Sydney and puzzled how the logistics could possibly work.

'Depends on what a person wants from their life, I guess. There are certainly more options and opportunities in the city.'

'With the rural economy not always buoyant, it becomes a lifestyle choice living out here, being at the mercy of the weather gods.' He glanced across the paddock where they worked, his gaze covering all the locals nearby digging and chatting sociably as they planted.

'Whoever lives in the country prefers the life and wants to be here.' She hoped he picked up on her commitment.

He stood up to dig the last of the tree holes in their section before lunch and Summer suspected that her hint was lost.

Jean and two other women plodded toward the lunch tent, unwrapping plates and baskets of food, and pouring hot drinks from the urn. It seemed to be a signal, for everyone hurriedly planted the last of their seedling tubes, set the plastic guards around them, washed their hands in the cold water from the tap at the back of the water tanker and headed for the tent.

The volunteers stood around in small clusters munching on fresh sandwiches and thickly buttered scones, nursing plastic cups of hot drinks. Ethan was the last to arrive. With two other men, he had packed up all the empty seedling trays and tools, stowing most of them in the back of his vehicle. After circulating and engaging most people in conversation while he ate, he collected a hot drink and joined Summer where she leant against a corner tent pole.

'You seem to be settling into the district well.'

'You don't listen — I did warn you.'

'Yes, you did.' He paused. 'Thanks for volunteering today.'

'I spend so much time alone on my property, so it's nice to get out and besides, I enjoyed it. I love seeing the land reward you for your efforts, and today was little effort.'

'Many hands certainly made light work.'

It was small talk but at least they weren't arguing, although conversation threatened to dry up until she braved a question. 'I notice Amos had a small supply of hay in his sheds from last season but it won't be enough to see me through the summer and autumn. Do you know someone in the district who might have a reliable supply of dry hay?'

His attention sharpened. 'Why do you need it? You don't have any livestock on your land.'

'I will have soon,' she replied.

'You planning on running sheep?'

She shook her head. 'Alpacas.' He raised his eyebrows but wisely stayed silent. 'They're great sheep guards, apparently. Maybe you could consider them for Karingal Park?' she teased, but then quickly bit her tongue. She must stop baiting him.

He shot her a look of mock disgust. 'I'm a sheep man.' He eyed her warily. 'You have experience with alpacas?'

'Some, yes, and I've just completed a course down near the coast at Jenny and Ross Peters' stud. I made plenty of contacts so there will be support and help if I need it.' To stall any further negative conversation on the subject when he scowled, she said, 'Getting back to the hay, do you know of anyone?'

'Your two lower paddocks would be worth mowing. Jean's son, Sean, does some independent contracting. He could use Amos' small tractor and slasher to save you some money.' He had given this thought while she was talking, and she felt bad for thinking ill of him again. 'I know for a fact it's been sitting in the machinery shed since last year. He'd probably be prepared to give you a lesson on basic maintenance and do a quick service. Be worth giving him a call.'

Just when she thought she had this man sorted, he tossed her another surprise. Why couldn't he always be like this? Maybe he was with everyone else. 'Thanks. I'll follow it up.'

'If you run low, I could let you have a regular supply.'

'Really? It needs to be quite dry. Mouldy hay can cause miscarriage in alpacas and I'll be breeding them eventually. Could you guarantee that?'

He stiffened and grew defensive. 'If you'd care to check out the quality first, you're welcome to come over and have a look for yourself.'

Summer knew the chance to see the homestead was not an opportunity to miss. It must be big if Sally Miller worked out there every weekend. She was not too proud to admit being nosy about where Ethan lived. With thousands of hectares and sheep, it should be worth seeing.

'You can call tomorrow. We'll be home all weekend,' he told her.

Summer noted he said 'we' and, our of pure curiosity, hoped she might meet his mother.

6

Sunday afternoon brought with it Summer's first visit to Karingal Park. Rattling in her van over the cattle grid between the impressive bluestone pillars at the bottom of the long driveway lined with aged pines should have been forewarning enough. But as she slowly cruised by lush green lawns, landscaped park-like gardens and mammoth ancient trees to draw up on the gravel at the front of the house, she actually gaped.

Because of its age, probably over one hundred years, the impressive double storey building had long since stamped its mark on the site. This was a mansion from the early and former glory days of sheep stations, the home of a pastoral dynasty.

Old money, gracious living and wealth were the words that came to Summer's mind. She couldn't help but compare her own mud brick cottage, with its rambling wildflower garden. Anyone else might have felt it came up short, yet Summer felt no envy. She merely wondered how anyone could need so much room — but the ancestor who built this clearly desired to flaunt his success and probably had a large family.

Summer's moment of awe and reflection was broken the instant she stepped from her van. A lovely black and cream kelpie raced toward her. No sign of Ethan, but if this was his dog, his master wouldn't be far away. She didn't have long to wait before Ethan strode around the corner of the house under the veranda, wearing his usual moleskins and checked shirt.

'Brewster, sit,' he commanded. The dog stopped a short distance away and sat on its haunches, eyeing her curiously, tongue hanging out and tail sweeping the gravel beneath him on the driveway.

'I was in my office and saw you arrive,' Ethan said as he took the front steps and came down to greet her.

Had he been waiting? 'Nice place,' she said with irony, tilting her head back and letting her gaze roam over the dark grey bluestone façade and crisp white timberwork around its windows. She warmed to his wide smile and their shared bond of humour that naturally flared between them.

'It's home.' He shrugged. 'I know we're fortunate to live here but we're really only caretakers for the next generation.'

'It's not too big for two people?'

'Mother and I rattle around a bit. Originally, of course, it housed my great great grandfather's family of seven children plus servants. None these days, of course, except Sally.'

'Quite a heritage.' Summer couldn't help but contrast his family's long term stability with the transient lifestyle of the Daltons.

'And a responsibility,' he replied. 'A huge pot of money goes into maintenance. Follow me.'

Getting straight down to business, he led her around the side of the house to a triple garage where his familiar Range Rover, a Holden utility and another sleek and expensive silver car were garaged. He opened the Ute door for Summer. Quick as a flash, Brewster jumped up into the back tray and Ethan chained him safely while she slid into the vehicle.

'Where I go, he goes,' Ethan grinned, glancing out the back cab window at the excited animal.

They drove through the house paddock and Ethan took Summer on a grand tour of the property. Vast endless pastures grazing countless numbers of sheep.

'What do you breed?'

'Because it's cooler than further inland most of the district flocks are superfine merinos that produce a dense, soft wool. We've only just finished shearing.'

'I'm going to need a shearer for my alpacas eventually. I'm not sure I have the strength to do it myself.'

'I could help with that,' Ethan said quietly.

'You know someone?'

'Yours truly. Can't be any harder than shearing a prize ram.'

Stunned by his increasing change of attitude, Summer snapped up his offer before he changed his mind. 'I'd pay, of course.'

'No need.' He grinned. 'But I might dream up suitable compensation.'

With the innuendo behind his deep voice, she realised he was flirting with her and, for the first time since her arrival, Summer saw a whole other side of Ethan Bourke. With the spectre of a girlfriend in the background, she didn't take his banter too seriously. But it revealed a lighter facet to his personality he hadn't shown before and it was impossible not to respond to his playful warmth.

Later, as they leaned over the timber railing fence of an inner yard surveying the distant green landscape dotted with freshly shorn white sheep, the caws of crows and shrieks of pink and grey galahs drifting across to them on the breeze, Summer asked, 'How do you keep your breeding flocks under control? You must have an upper limit that you can graze on the property.'

'Average lifespan is about thirteen years but around the age of five or six we do an annual cull of the ewes that are beyond breeding age.'

A gust of wind from behind them caught Summer's spread of long hair and blew it in a raven mist across her shoulders. She knew Ethan had been watching her because she felt his gaze even without looking. Out of interest, when she turned to meet his eyes, she saw the ruffled hair, the look of contentment on his face, and knew this was where he belonged. But before he turned away, she also saw his jaw clench and a look of longing that was so swiftly checked she wondered if she had imagined it.

'What are you thinking?' she dared to ask.

'That you're asking some knowledge-able questions for someone who's only recently moved to the country. Not all women want to live in the bush, even those that were raised here, so I'm betting you've never been a city girl.'

Summer gave a gentle reminiscent smile. 'No. As I was growing up, I worked alongside David and absorbed every piece of information he passed on to me about his organic gardening practices, and recently I did some study on my own. A Diploma of Agriculture externally through the University of New England in Armidale.'

'Northern New South Wales,' Ethan murmured in thought. 'Close to where you live.'

'Not too far. It gave me a basic knowledge of agriculture and sustain-able production.'

'What made you decide to do it?'

'I'd always wanted a few acres of my own. What about you? When you left school did you come straight out onto the farm?'

Ethan shook his head. 'No. After private school in Hamilton and Geelong, I did a degree in agricultural business management.'

'But you must have learned a lot from growing up here.'

He nodded. 'My grandfather, Alexander Winslow, had an encyclopaedic knowledge of sheep. Knew the history of every ewe on the property. And my father was a shearer.'

Summer was amazed to hear it. Victoria Winslow fell in love with a workman? Fascinating — and it set Summer to wondering if it was in rebellion or genuinely for love. 'You talk about him in the past tense.'

Ethan clenched his jaw and his narrowed gaze slid toward the horizon. 'He died many years ago.'

'How do you manage?'

He didn't answer for a while and eventually admitted, 'It gets hectic at times, but I have a full time man, Jack. He's a friend more than a worker.'

Summer could imagine. Once you

got to know him, Ethan Bourke wasn't the starchy autocrat of first impressions. He was a down to earth bloke who was born on the land and loved it. Too serious, maybe, but she was willing to bet that out of his diligence he always gave one hundred per cent to everything he did.

Small things mattered to him and while she might find it fussy, she guessed it stemmed from a need for perfection. In hindsight, she realised what she had previously considered criticisms from him might well have been comments made out of experience and neighbourly concern.

'Does your mother take any part in helping run the property?'

Ethan's sober face broke into an abandoned smile. 'Victoria? No. It would be great if she was more interested but she's misplaced. She should be living in Melbourne. After my father died, I thought she'd move but she needed the security of living here. I presumed it would only be for a while but it's been ten years now and she's growing unhappier with every passing year.'

Summer appreciated that he took her into his confidence with personal family matters. She hadn't even met the woman but already felt sorry for her. 'She doesn't type or do the books?'

Ethan chuckled. 'No. She wouldn't even know how to turn on a computer let alone operate it. Not her fault really. She was raised to have everything done for her and still expects it.' He let out a long sigh. 'No, my mother would rather go shopping, dress up, socialise. The country isolation is getting to her. She doesn't have many friends on what she considers her social level so she's finding it hard.'

'That's such a pity.'

'I've tried to encourage her to move into our apartment in the city but so far she's refused.'

'Why, when she's so unhappy?'

'Mother comes from a generation and a family who apparently hid their feelings so, although she doesn't give the impression, I believe she's reluctant to leave while I remain . . . unattached.' He pulled a wry grin. 'Meanwhile, she stays and gets more restless every day.'

'Family.' Summer gave a long sigh. 'They're difficult to live with sometimes, but where would we be without them? They're usually the one constant in our lives. I really wish there hadn't been the rift in our family so I could have known Amos, too.'

To her surprise, Ethan took her hand in his and linked fingers. 'I don't want to make you feel worse but he was a great old bloke. He was like a surrogate grandfather to me after old Alexander died.'

'You must have known him well. I don't suppose he ever mentioned that he wanted a reconciliation with my father?' she asked warily.

'Not in so many words but, do you know, I believe deep down he probably did. But if you'll forgive my honesty, he was a stubborn old beggar and I can only assume his fierce pride wouldn't let him make the first move. No consolation to you now, I guess, but I think Amos deeply regretted pushing David out of his life.'

Summer shrugged. 'Farming is my father's life. He just sought a less conventional way of going about it.'

'He was no different to most of his generation at the time,' Ethan granted. 'Amos lived by a stricter sense of morals than those of the liberal Seventies. Our parents pushed the boundaries of what was acceptable. As Amos grew older, I gained the impression that he felt it was too late to repair the damage.'

'With David being an only child, I wish they had both made an effort. He probably died a fairly lonely man. He could have had his son and grandchildren in his life. Even if he didn't agree with my father's choice of permissive lifestyle, he could at least have stayed in touch.'

'I was only young at the time when it all happened, not yet a teenager, but I remember overhearing my parents talk. For a while there was gossip about the black sheep Dalton son who got a girl pregnant, lived together instead of marrying and was thrown out by his father. I'm sure it was a time of conflict and rebellion in many families. Society was on the threshold of a new era; kids openly defied their parents, snubbed their noses at tradition and did their own thing.'

Ethan was quiet for a moment before he continued quietly, 'I believe in the tradition of marriage, the possibility of a true and lasting love, the security of trusting and relying on each other. Marriage is still the backbone of society. Life revolves around the family unit and the support and love it provides. Or should . . . '

Although she knew her parents' lifestyle was alternative rather than traditional and not what she wanted for herself, Summer found herself defending them. 'I know my parents' open relationships aren't for everyone but they're adults and they have the right to live the life they choose for themselves, even if others don't agree. If it doesn't bother either of them, I don't think it's anyone's concern but theirs. I have five half brothers and sisters, all younger than me.'

'Really?'

Summer nodded. She wasn't sure if Ethan was genuinely interested or surprised. 'Yes. Skye, Willow and Magnolia are the girls, and, River and Quinn are the boys. Do you have any siblings?'

Ethan released her hand and moved away from the fence, sinking his hands into his pockets. 'I had a younger brother,' he revealed uneasily.

At the sadness in his voice and because he spoke in the past tense again, Summer was about to probe further when a chill wind whipped by them and she shivered, instinctively edging closer to him for warmth.

'Are you cold?' His focus strayed from their conversation to concern for her comfort.

'Not really. I guess I'll have to get used to fresh breezes after living in the subtropics all my life.'

'So you're settling here permanently?'

She sent him a suspicious glare. 'I know where this is going.'

He shrugged, grinning, and the shadow of darkness that had previously etched his face softened. 'Offer's always open. If you need it.'

'Thanks, but no thanks.' She looked out over the peaceful countryside again. 'I'm growing to love it here. Well,' she turned to him, rubbing her chilled hands together, 'I've seen your prize rams and breeding ewes and had the grand tour but I did come here to look at your hay.'

'Sure.' He opened the Ute door for her. 'Then I'll take you up to the house to meet my mother.'

They bumped over grassy tracks toward a massive open-sided hay shed stacked from the ground to the roof with huge bales.

'Doesn't look like you'll run out any

time soon,' Summer quipped.

Ethan grinned. 'We had a good season. We always keep a certain amount on hand and sell the rest. After mowing we let it stand until it's the right water content then bale it in the warmest part of the day, so there shouldn't be a problem with mould. But just watch out for it when you split them open at feeding. If there's a problem, just let me know and I'll replace it.'

'Thanks.' Summer was genuinely grateful.

'Are you going to be able to handle the bales?' He eyed her in dubious speculation.

She glanced across at him in amusement. 'I might look like a pixie but I have the strength of a Clydesdale. All the same, those bales do look awesome and I'll probably need a pair of strong arms to help.'

'Sure. Just say the word.'

He seemed to relax with the quiet openness that had developed between them, which surprised her, especially since she hadn't received the warmest welcome from him when she first arrived.

'When would you like the hay delivered?'

'As the buyer, I guess I'm supposed to collect them but I notice Amos didn't own a trailer. I'm guessing eventually I might need one and learn how to tow and back the darn thing.'

Ethan chuckled in good humour. 'Not a problem. You're only five minutes down the road.'

'There's no hurry. I won't have my animals until after I visit the alpaca field day and auction down on the Peters' property soon. Ross said he'd help me select three or four of the most suitable to start my herd.'

'I'll drop the hay over in a few days, then.'

'Great.' She broached the subject of price and payment, a touchy area with her limited funds. 'I have the money. I just need to keep a tight rein on it until

I'm earning from the property and my grandfather's estate is properly settled.'

'No problem,' he said easily. 'Pay me when you can.' Then he said some words that warmed her heart and rewarded her tolerance in getting to know him. 'I trust you.'

His belief in her filled her with elation. She wondered if it extended to her capability to run Greenbanks. 'Thanks.'

'You're most welcome.' His broad smile competed with the sunshine for lighting up the day. 'Let's head back to the house.'

As they reached the homestead again, a tall, willowy, middle-aged woman stood on the front steps looking anxious and pacing. Summer immediately felt Ethan stiffen as tension began to build beside her in the Ute cabin. With a kind of leashed patience, he slid out of the Ute, opened Summer's door, untied Brewster and, with the dog trotting adoringly at his heels, strode toward the house.

Summer followed behind, looking around his big frame at the woman with a sharp nose in an otherwise lovely face and deep crinkles at the corner of her eyes that pierced her with a cold glare over Ethan's shoulder. To Summer, her slacks and shirt looked tailored and her bleached short hair was immaculately styled back from her face.

'Everything all right, Mother?' Summer noticed the measured tone of Ethan's voice.

'Where have you been?' she snapped. Although she spoke to Ethan, her gaze rested severely on Summer.

'Taking Summer around the property. Is there a problem? You could have reached me on the radio.'

'You know I don't like using that thing. And keep that animal out of my house.' She glared harshly at Brewster.

'I always do, Mother,' he said, deliberately patient.

Summer's first thoughts were how on earth Ethan lived in any kind of peace and harmony with this harridan of a woman, and how anyone could not love his beautiful, intelligent dog. Summer bent down to pat his head and affectionately play with his ear.

When Ethan turned aside to Summer, he noticed her affection to Brewster. The tenderness that softened his face and his wickedly knowing half smile told her they shared a special secret moment. Crazy as it seemed and against her will, Summer realised that she couldn't help liking the man.

Taking a gentle hold of her elbow and drawing her forward, Ethan said, 'Mother, this is Summer Dalton. Amos' grand-daughter. She's moved into Greenbanks.'

'Yes, I know, you told me. Ms Dalton.' She inclined her head and ran a judgmental eye from the top of Summer's glossy black hair, the long thin jumper over a cotton skirt, to the gold anklet with its butterfly charm and the scruffy sandals on her feet. Summer was left in no doubt that she was considered inadequate.

'Summer, this is my mother, Victoria,'

Ethan muttered, not sounding particularly thrilled by his mother's hostile manner.

'I'm really pleased to meet you, Victoria,' Summer replied politely, but the woman's look of astonishment told her that perhaps using her first name had been too familiar. When Summer extended a hand in greeting Victoria looked at it with disdain, ignored it and spun around.

'I have an appointment shortly. I can't stay,' she said imperiously, her back to them as she climbed the steps to the front porch, leaving Summer feeling as if they had just been dismissed.

'You didn't need to wait around, Mother. You could have left a note,' Ethan called after her but Summer doubted his mother heard, for the front door slammed behind her as she disappeared from sight.

Ethan turned to her and pulled a stiff smile. She sensed restrained fury seeping from him from every pore. 'I should be able to deliver the hay on Tuesday,' he told her.

'Brilliant. I'll see you then. Thanks for the tour. Peace,' she said softly as she left, then clambered into her van and drove away, aching with compassion over the difficult life Ethan must lead, living with Victoria in the same house.

Sam had said he came with emotional baggage. She realised now he had probably meant Ethan's mother. When her thoughts became charitable again, she realised that every unhappiness had a root cause and she would love to know what had happened in the Bourke household that made them all so miserable.

7

Ethan's Ute arrived two days later in a familiar cloud of dust with its deep, powerful engine throbbing up the track from the road. Her hay bales were stacked two high on its tray.

Working outdoors, Summer saw him arrive and wandered across to greet him. As he unwound his tall frame from the vehicle and stretched, Summer was impressed. He was a good-looking specimen of a man but she puzzled over the spark and camaraderie developing between them. If this continued, they might even become friends.

In contrast to the first time they'd met when she wasn't troubled if she never saw him again, she now looked forward to seeing him any time and for any reason.

'Morning.' She removed her black floppy hat and loosened her hair, damp with perspiration, to let the hint of a breeze cool her down a little. 'Can you take them over to the storage shed beyond the house?'

'Sure. Jump in.'

They drove down to the shed and Summer watched in awe as Ethan unlatched the Ute tray and with effortless brawny strength hauled the bales inside. She managed to push one from the Ute onto the ground and drag it to join the others, but when she struggled to stack it into position following Ethan's lead, the twine broke open, hay spilt everywhere and she tumbled into the midst of it all.

She sat up, laughing, and took Ethan's hands as he helped her up.

'You're not hurt?' he asked.

She shook her head and laughed again. 'Only my pride.'

Still holding one hand, he released the other and carefully plucked blades of straw from her hair and clothes. Standing close together, their heavy breathing from lugging bales of hay the only sound around them, Summer sensed a deeper awareness spring into life.

Ethan stilled and stared down at her. For a moment she thought and hoped that he might kiss her, but he snapped out of his trance and murmured, 'There. You're looking respectable again.'

Summer decided to push his boundaries. 'Around you, I'm not entirely sure I want to be.'

Far from being shocked by her suggestive comment, Ethan gave her a cautious glance. 'You're far too enticing for your own good, Miss Dalton,' he said with dangerous softness.

'News to me,' she said lightly and meant it.

After a moment, he added, 'You're the kind of woman men find themselves wanting to protect.'

Summer found his observation surprising because, from childhood, she'd pretty much had to look out for herself. 'Not so far in my life, they haven't.' She pulled an ironic grin.

He paused before dragging the next

bale off the vehicle. 'Then maybe you haven't met a real man yet.'

If that was a challenge, she was up for it, so when they finished, she offered, 'Stay for a cool drink?'

He pushed back his Akubra to wipe the sweat from his brow before settling it back low over his forehead again. He hesitated before shaking his head. 'Sorry. Duty calls.'

Suddenly the companionship and camaraderie was gone and a wall of distance was erected again. Feeling awkward, pretending she wasn't bothered by his change of mood, Summer said, 'Sure, okay.'

She couldn't deny her disappointment. After all, even though Ethan did have a girlfriend, their relationship was casual and conducted long distance; he was bound to be attracted to other women. Her fault. She shouldn't have teased him for a reaction. But he had flirted with her and seemed to enjoy her company.

'Thanks for the hay,' she said sharply.

'Send me an account and I'll get the first payment to you when I can. Peace.'

Ethan climbed back into the Ute and gave her a weak smile and a wave through his open window before he gunned the car into life and drove away. Disheartened, Summer steeled herself to be snubbed again in the future. She was new in the district and she'd briefly caught his attention and, after his initial hostility, had managed to become friends. From his side, she mustn't expect anything more, no matter how much she might wish it to be different.

★ ★ ★

Later that week, Summer made a phone call to her immediate neighbour. 'Hi Sam. How have you been?'

'Rheumatism's playing up,' he grumbled. 'Rain must be coming.'

Summer knew better than to dismiss or ridicule his prediction. Old timers knew the weather and seasons backed by a lifetime of experience. 'Hope not. I haven't fixed my roof yet.'

'We've been known to get some decent summer thunderstorms even this early in the summer.'

It was more than she wanted to hear. 'I'm just confirming that you and your trailer are still coming down with me on Saturday to the coast for the alpaca field day and auction.'

'Well now, girlie.' Sam's hesitation put Summer on alert. 'I was backing the trailer the other day after I'd loaded some lambs but I put the Ute into reverse instead of drive and it shot into my concrete rainwater tank and buckled the back of it. Red's got it in the garage to repair. Eyesight's not what it used to be,' he muttered with an apology.

'Are you and the lambs okay?' Summer asked with concern.

'Yeah, the animals are all right but the doc put one of them foam thingies around my neck. Whiplash, he reckons. Gotta take it easy for a few days. But I could still come down with you,' he added bravely.

'No, absolutely not.' Her mind scrambled over how she would get herself out of a tight corner. As though it didn't matter and Sam's accident hadn't completely thrown out her plans, she said brightly, 'I made marmalade yesterday. I'll bring some over for you.'

'Don't like the runny stuff,' he mumbled.

Summer grinned to herself. 'You can cut it with a knife and it spreads like jelly,' she told him.

'Pleased to hear it. Nothing worse than jam that runs off your bread.'

Although their conversation ended with humour, when Summer hung up on the call, she knew she was in a predicament. Somehow, from somewhere, she needed a trailer to bring home her alpacas — but she couldn't afford to buy one.

There was another option, of course, but she hesitated to consider it. Exhausting the alternative and hating herself for relying on him so much, Summer swallowed her pride and picked up the phone for a second call.

'Karingal Park.' Victoria's cultured voice came down the line.

Summer hadn't expected Ethan would necessarily be at the house. He could be anywhere on the property, so the odds were high that she would speak to his mother. She introduced herself and asked for Ethan.

Victoria responded crisply and sparsely with, 'He's not at home.'

'Could you ask him to call me when he has a chance, please?'

'If I remember.'

She couldn't write herself a note, Summer thought? 'I'd appreciate it.'

The suspension of waiting kept Summer edgy. She didn't want Ethan to think her a helpless female or pressing some kind of unwanted female advantage; she had a genuine need of his help.

Normally calm and slow to be ruffled, Summer paced the house and garden for hours before he returned her call later that morning.

On hearing his deep voice at the other end of the line, she took a deep breath and explained her dilemma, running on quickly to add, 'I know it's a big ask and I don't have a tow ball on the van — '

'Not a problem.' Stunned by his easy agreement, she fell silent. 'Consider it done,' he went on. 'I'll drive you down, in case you need a strong pair of hands.'

'I hate to put you to any trouble again. I didn't expect you to. It will be a full day thing,' she rambled.

'You're never any trouble, Summer,' he said. 'I'll make myself free.'

Such co-operation and flattery. He was being super nice and she grew suspicious after his rebuff the other day out in the hay shed. Perhaps he was just being neighbourly.

* * *

Ethan pulled his four-wheel drive and trailer to a stop outside Greenbanks cottage. Laddie was playing outside and bounded enthusiastically toward him.

'Hey, boy.' He stooped to pat him as

he approached the house. Remembering to duck under the wind chimes
hanging along the length of the veranda
and tinkling in the warm summer
breeze, he walked up to the front door.
He knocked but there was no response.

In the country, if you knew the
owners and the door was open, you
simply went in. He took the initiative
and entered the unlocked cottage. His
nostrils flared with appreciation. Cinna-
mon? Summer always seemed to be
baking something.

He heard her soft melodic voice from
further off in the cottage. Sounded like
she was on the phone. While he waited,
he paced the living room. It was not so
much untidy as lived-in. An afghan
was tossed over the back of the sofa. A
large square cushion sat on the floor,
indented. It didn't surprise him that she
preferred sitting there. Misty appeared
from somewhere in the house and frisked
over to him, rubbing herself against his
ankles and purring.

Ethan cursed himself for taking

advantage of any excuse to visit or spend time with Summer. Initially he told himself he was doing what he promised Amos and watching out for his farm, but he sure didn't need to do that any more. Summer was proving herself a competent landowner. Beneath her green fingers; the garden had been rejuvenated and transformed, produce from vegetable beds was thriving. She certainly had no problem with hard work and getting her hands dirty.

His thoughts grew philosophical. Neither his mother nor Meredith had any interest in the outdoors. Victoria preferred a lazy social life while Meredith's efforts were fully concentrated on her publicity career in Sydney. She loved the limelight, something he shunned, and that aspect of their lifetime friendship bothered him.

It was impossible not to compare the women who had been a major part of his life, if not an influence. He'd always regretted Meredith's stubborn partiality for the city, and now realised that was where she was meant to be.

Whereas Summer Dalton, he thought, as he sank his hands into his pockets and looked around the homely room, was meant to be here.

He could hear Summer's laughter and chatter. Whoever she was speaking to, she knew them well. Curious and hating himself for eavesdropping, he moved further across the living room. The office door was ajar so her voice echoed and travelled down the hall.

'I can't wait to see you again either. I know. I miss you too, sweetheart.' There was a pause. 'I love you, too.'

With such intimate endearments, the person on the other end of the phone had to be a boyfriend. The realisation brought him up with a sudden jolt. He hadn't for a moment even considered that there might be anyone else in Summer's life. Naïve and blinkered of him. He cursed as envy ate into his gut.

He heard her murmur sad goodbyes then hang up. Moments later she emerged, smiling and humming, and he secretly watched her in the seconds before she noticed him. She was still as lithe and gangly as when she'd arrived, but she'd browned up. Her skin now glowed golden, her dark hair swung in a silky cloud over her shoulders and back. She had been a breath of fresh air in his life and the district.

As he stood quietly across the room, Summer's preoccupation passed and she noticed him. 'Oh, hello, there. I didn't hear you come in. I was just on the phone.'

'Sounds like someone special.'

'The love of my life,' she readily admitted with a deep happy sigh.

Her bluntly honest admission made him take an emotional step back. Damn near impossible, when she looked so engaging in the floppy cotton trousers she always seemed to wear and long, blue tie-dyed shirt that highlighted the colour of her eyes. Even in the unflattering baggy style she looked serenely feminine.

Her easygoing manner filled him with

envy and annoyance. Nothing bothered her. She never wore a watch and the grandfather clock in the hall hadn't been rewound. Yet despite being so breezy and competent, he found himself wanting to keep her safe, be around to help her. When she'd phoned two days ago, the protective male side of him had kicked into gear. Now with this new information of someone important in her life, it looked like he didn't need to bother. He'd misread her signals.

'I didn't keep you waiting too long?'

Summer's words drew him back. 'No, not at all. Ready for the day?' he asked more lightly than he felt.

'Absolutely. And excited. Ross is going to help me choose my alpacas today and I get to bring them home.' Ethan was charmed by her uncomplicated, childish delight. 'The start of my flock.'

A waft of lavender drifted with her as she walked past.

★　★　★

Speeding along the minor road toward the coastal village of Port Fairy, Ethan's trailer rattling on behind, Summer gazed out of the vehicle window and said, 'The scenery and life down here is so different to back home . . . I mean, up north,' she corrected, grinning. 'They're coming into the steamy wet season now.'

'Which do you prefer?'

'This sheep country grows on you.' She didn't add that also included the people. 'I'm looking forward to settling and raising my family here. My childhood was filled with independence and freedom but I always felt like I was more part of a wider community, not in a close family unit.

'Plus I was always helping raise younger siblings,' she went on easily. 'It was a mixed-up family life. Looking back, I guess I was a little lost and confused, not quite accepting it all but never bothering to question. I don't want that for my children. I want them to have a stable life. Taking up

Greenbanks gives me that chance. You have no idea what a gift that was and how much it means to me.'

Ethan gave a soft whistle. 'I really blundered in there with my offer to buy the place then, didn't I?'

'I'm sure your heart was in the right place but you're always so full of advice and taking control. Well meant, I'm sure,' she added hastily, glancing at him in the hope he wasn't offended by her judgment. Her shoulders sagged in relief to see a soft smile of amusement on his face. 'But I don't know you well, and it does make me wonder why,' she ended, leaving a huge and unsubtle opening for him to elaborate.

'I guess I'm used to the women in my life being so dependent. Leaving decisions to me. They're not enthusiastic, competent farmers like you.'

'Ethan.' Summer placed a hand on her chest, pretending shock. 'Not a compliment, surely?'

He shrugged and the corners of his eyes wrinkled with humour. 'Just stating a fact.' He kept his gaze firmly fixed on the road ahead. 'You either love the country or you don't.'

'I agree. You know, money and material possessions mean nothing to me. What's more important to me above everything is a secure sense of family. I accept the way my parents live, but that uncommitted situation isn't for me. I have a daughter to consider.'

'You're in a relationship?'

'No.' Although she hesitated, she figured it couldn't hurt to elaborate, so she explained about the whole Billy thing, being deserted to manage alone. 'When we were partners, he promised we would marry. He knew it was important to me but when I became pregnant with Ivy, he broke his promise and shot through.'

'I'm sorry to hear that.'

He certainly didn't sound like it. In fact, he looked rather pleased with himself. Maybe he was just happy to be talking, unloading, sharing . . .

'I guess I was just a bit too naïve back

then,' she admitted readily.

'Life throws good times and bad at everyone,' Ethan agreed. 'My father was a gun shearer when he met my mother. He was a charming, handsome womaniser who loved fun. Mother was captivated. He was different and exciting. All the men she'd met until then were probably sons of socially acceptable families. My father broke all the rules. He was a rough outdoor man, used to living and playing hard.' Ethan paused. 'He loved to drink, too, so I guess my mother figured it was a perfect opportunity to defy her parents.

'After they married, Victoria assumed Richard would give up shearing to manage the property but he was unhappy at being forced to conform and refused. He couldn't deal with being harassed by his ambitious father-in-law. Old Alexander Winslow apparently claimed he wasn't good enough for his daughter. So my father took to drink more and more.

'He kept shearing but probably only

because it took him away from home. He neglected Karingal Park until Alex died, then he was forced to return. My parents' resentment of each other meant there was no harmony in the house and their marriage crumbled.

'Richard was a strong, good-looking man but emotionally weak. He had a couple of affairs, became an alcoholic, and . . . well, he was drunk when he drove the car that killed him and my younger brother, Simon.'

'Oh, God,' Summer breathed, her heart going out to him. Her hand instinctively reached across to touch his arm.

'Ten years ago,' Ethan went on. 'I had just started university. Mother wanted me to come home to the property but I just couldn't bear to be alone in that big house with only her so we put in a manager, Jack Oliver . . . I mentioned him before.' Summer nodded. 'He still works with me. I finished my course and went back two years later.

'That's about when I drifted toward

your grandfather. Jack's a great bloke but he's good with sheep, not words. Besides, he has a big family and I didn't want to burden him. So Amos became my mentor. He was strong to the point of being stubborn but we respected each other and became good friends as well as neighbours. I watched out for him as he grew older. I dropped by Greenbanks every day . . . '

He paused and an almost uncomfortable silence fell between them.

'I found Amos when he died,' he told her gently, his jaw clenched.

Summer drew in a shocked gasp. 'I didn't know.' She acquired a raised respect for this man who had been through enough with his own family, but then to find her grandfather . . .

'It must have been so hard for you visiting Greenbanks afterwards and seeing it empty and quiet.'

'It was, but I'd promised him I would keep an eye on the place. Even now whenever I walk into the cottage, it's like a second home.'

'Really?' His confession inexplicably filled her with happiness. 'I hope you'll always feel like that. I know Amos isn't there any more, but . . . '

'While you're there, Summer, it will always hold warm memories.'

For a while they fell silent and the hum of tyres on the road was the only sound between them until Ethan spoke again. 'With my father's poor management, Karingal Park was run down, but Jack and I managed to build it up again into the successful stud merino property it used to be. I want to see it left in good hands for my own sons one day.'

Summer felt uplifted that Ethan had confided in her about his family life. Despite the tragedy, he seemed quietly confident and proud of his achievements and looking forward to the future.

It was only an hour's journey from Wombat Creek to the coast but to Summer it seemed much shorter because she and Ethan chatted all the way, making the trip fly.

Soon they were turning down a familiar sealed side road before reaching Port Fairy village, and headed toward the Peters' alpaca stud breeding property. A paddock at the front had been recently mowed and was already half full with rows of cars. Crowds of milling people around tents and in small paddocks close to the homestead were already viewing the animals on show for the day and talking business.

Ethan parked his vehicle and trailer at the side of the field for easy departure later when they needed to load her animals.

Pressing down a building excitement that the day had actually arrived when she would buy her first breeding stock, she trudged happily alongside Ethan as they stepped through lush ankle-high grass together toward an information tent at the gate in the nearest fence. Summer put her name down for a time slot appointment with Ross and Jenny later to choose her animals. Their entry tickets put them into a lucky door prize for a free alpaca mating.

'Could come in handy,' Ethan murmured.

Summer glanced across at him, about to make a responding quip, expecting his comment would be laced with humour, but he was frowning and quite serious. His vast experience with stud animals had come to the fore and, for him, this was all about business, so she sobered.

'Absolutely. If I win,' she agreed, trying to keep a straight face.

They joined the keen throngs of fellow attendees and turned their attention to the display and catering tents. With a piping hot drink and sandwich each, they ate and drank as they strolled about.

Summer found a huge craft tent with an overwhelming display of beautiful, soft garments made by alpaca spinners and weavers. All manner of clothing and products were for sale; throw rugs, shawls, jumpers. Even alpaca fleece in doonas and pillows.

Forgetting Ethan in her bliss, she instantly plunged into excited conversation with stallholders and women working at their crafts, gleaning tips. When she realised much later that he was missing, she scanned the crowds and noticed him patiently leaning against a tent pole nearby and gazing off distractedly into the distance.

'I hope you won't be too bored.' Summer expressed her concern after sauntering over to him. On the way, she had secretly admired the tall, handsome man with his sandy hair half-hidden beneath his familiar broad-brimmed hat. Most of the women spared second glances as they strolled past. If they spoke, he touched the brim of his hat in greeting. Of course she had never met Richard Bourke, but it seemed Ethan had inherited some of his father's devilish charm.

He straightened and flashed her an easy, brilliant smile. 'It's a whole different world to sheep, that's for sure.'

'There are some gorgeous jumpers

and shawls in there your mother might appreciate,' she suggested.

After a late lunch of homemade vegetable soup and a wholemeal roll, it was time for Summer's appointment with the Peters. Unable to control her enthusiasm, she strode ahead of Ethan back to the information tent at the gate where it had been arranged they should meet.

Jenny was waiting, dressed in her usual jeans and blue checked shirt with their property logo embroidered on the top pocket.

'Hi, Summer. Great to see you again,' she greeted her warmly.

'Jen, this is my neighbour, Ethan Bourke.'

As they shook hands, Summer didn't miss the other woman's admiring glance. Then, grinning, Jenny said to Summer, 'Ready to choose your animals?' Summer nodded. 'Great. Peter's in the yard waiting. We've culled out what we consider the most suitable for your needs, judging by what you told us at the weekend workshop.'

There were further introductions all around when they met Peter in the yard but Summer couldn't keep her eyes off the beautiful alpacas they had chosen with their long necks and legs, soft wool bodies and adorably sweet faces.

'Based on what you've told us, I think you said your main objective was for breeding but with fibre for your own spinning, so these should all fit into that category. We'd suggest a bred female, another young female and a wethered companion.'

Summer's interest focused on a dark fawn female. Noticing her appreciation, Jen smiled. 'She has a beautiful temperament and soft handling fleece. She's already been mated with a black sire and is due to give birth soon. She'll cost more, but it will give a boost to your initial herd and be a sound long term financial investment.'

Summer frowned, running some quick financial calculations through her head. Quietly observant, Jen said,

'There are a few owners locally who need agistment for their animals. I can put you in touch with them, if you like. It's all extra income.'

'Great.' Summer smiled with relief. 'I'd appreciate that.'

Ross led over a couple of wethered and haltered companion animals. When Summer had made her choice, she tossed a questioning glance across at Ethan where he stood against the fence. He nodded and she returned his smile.

'Looks like you've made your decision,' Ross chuckled. 'You'll find with time you'll get to know their personalities. They're intelligent and easy to love, especially the cria when it's born.'

'At the workshop, you mentioned the females are fertile for up to fifteen years. How old is my bred female?'

'She's five now and can be bred again at any time. Same with the other young female you choose.'

'I'm rather attracted to that one.' Summer pointed out a lighter cream fleeced animal.

With her selections made, Summer and Ethan had free time until the Peters and their staff could separate and settle the animals she had chosen into smaller yarding pens ready for loading.

'We could head into Port Fairy for a look round?' Ethan suggested.

Summer beamed her approval and strode off toward his vehicle, looking forward to some down time.

Since her arrival, her life seemed all about working to get Greenbanks up and running again. With the acquisition of her first animals, that process was nearly complete and she could give consideration to when and how she could bring Ivy down to join her.

8

Ethan unhooked the trailer and left it in the paddock. Within ten minutes, they were driving the streets of the small historic tourist village and admiring the beautifully restored stone settlers' cottages where daisies and lavender peeped through picket fences, old Georgian style buildings stood grand and proud, and a bluestone flour mill was now converted into a boutique hotel.

'Whalers and sealers established one of the earliest ports here,' Ethan told her. 'In the early 1800s the cutter Fairy was driven into the port by bad weather and that's how the town got its name. This whole stretch of coastline is notorious for shipwrecks.'

Summer was impressed by the delightful fishing village steeped in history and nestling on the banks of the picturesque Moyne River. Ethan drove down to the water and parked. They wandered along the wharf where anglers sat perched on the boardwalk with lines dangling in the water and commercial fishing boats were returning with the day's catch.

Summer longingly eyed the crates of lobster being unloaded. She loved seafood, but could rarely afford such a luxury.

Absorbed in the bustle of activity, she didn't notice Ethan missing until she turned to make a comment and he wasn't there. She scanned the vicinity until she noticed him in a small fresh fish shop nearby.

He returned holding a big bag with red claws and feelers sticking out of one end. 'I noticed how longingly you looked at them,' he said. 'Thought it might be nice to swing by the bakery and eat it with the local specialty whaler's loaf.' He hesitated. 'I don't drink, but I could buy a bottle of wine for you.'

His statement caught her by surprise,

but she held his gaze and recovered, guessing the reason why.

'I don't either,' she told him honestly. 'I think they'll be perfect on their own, don't you? A hot cuppa is on me later when we get home.'

He gave her a heart-stopping smile and murmured, 'Deal.'

Feeling a positive sense of promise spring into life between them and nervous about where it might lead, they strolled to the bakery, picked up the bread and walked across the causeway at one end of town that led to a lighthouse and beaches on Griffiths Island. Ethan had collected a rug from his vehicle on the way which he spread out on the sand.

As they sat together pulling apart the succulent white lobster flesh and mopping up the juices with chunks of bread, the sun sank behind them creating a vivid orange sky. It was impossible not to notice the thousands of birds nesting on the small island.

Ethan caught her fascinated gaze.

'Mutton birds. They're protected in Victoria. Tens of thousands return here to the nesting grounds on almost the same day in September each year.'

She grinned. 'You're kidding?' When he shook his head, she added, 'That's awesome.'

'Every year they make a fifteen thousand kilometre flight of migration across the Pacific Ocean.'

'How do they survive?'

Ethan shrugged. 'Nature, I guess. The adult birds leave in autumn about mid April, but the young stay behind. Somehow they find the right route without their parents when hunger drives them from the nest. The fidelity of the adults is renowned. They return to the same nesting burrow every year and usually stay with the same mate for life.'

Summer listened in awe, aware of Ethan sitting beside her, his big shoulder touching hers and the swift glance of meaning he tossed her as he spoke. 'They've already mated in November, then the birds fly off for a two week honeymoon at sea.'

'Who knew birds would be so romantic?' Summer sighed, her thoughts turning dreamy.

Ethan chuckled. 'They've laid an egg and each pair shares incubation duties until it hatches in January. You should hear the noise.' He shook his head. 'The parents head out to sea for food every day and there's a great spectacle at sunset when they return to shore to feed their young.'

'I must come back then to see it.'

'When I was growing up, we came here often every summer. It really is a great sight.'

Summer hugged her knees against the fresh breeze off the gently lapping water. 'You said they migrate in April. Do you know where they go?' she asked.

'They pass New Zealand, then head up to Japan and on to their wintering grounds around the Aleutian Islands near Alaska. The prevailing winds help them and they do it in about two months, but when they head south again and come down the coast of California, they have to battle against the winds across the Pacific.'

'They must be exhausted.'

'I'm sure they are.'

'It's a miracle how each bird can find its mate among all the others in the colony,' Summer reflected, almost to herself. 'The mysteries of wildlife. I knew swans mated for life. I guess there are heaps of other species that do the same. Humans aren't so unique in wanting the same thing, are they?'

'Seems not. I imagine it's kind of special finding that one person you want to be with for life.'

'Not to mention it being a challenge.' She glanced across at him, thinking of what the locals had told her about Meredith. 'Have you ever come close to finding anyone?'

'No one definite. My mother has her own ideas, of course. Very strong ones, as you can imagine after meeting her. But she's had first-hand experience of the heartbreak, because my grand-parents considered she married beneath her. She's determined that I should marry someone of what she considers our own social class. Whatever that is,' he muttered.

'She organises dinner parties and I allow myself to be dragged along to her charity events, where she sits me next to potential ladies,' he went on. 'But after seeing my parents' mismatch, it makes you think more deeply about the most suitable person to spend your life with. You need to consider the other person's needs and make sacrifices so the relationship is a mutual fit.'

'Anyone special in your life?' Summer hated herself for fishing. More accus-tomed to being blunt and up front, being devious wasn't usually her thing and didn't come naturally.

'Ah, the local grapevine,' Ethan chuckled. 'I presume you're referring to the lovely Meredith Wells?'

'I have heard her name mentioned . . . '

'We grew up together. As teenagers

in school holidays, we were always on horses and motorbikes somewhere on Karingal Park or her parents' property, next door. The other side from your place.'

'Is she still in the district?'

Ethan shook his head. 'No. She's a Sydney girl these days.'

'So, how is that going to work for you two then?'

'Not sure. There used to be a connection . . . ' He shrugged and trailed off. 'Seeing the disaster of my parents' marriage unfold, you realise there are no guarantees. The right person needs to fit into your lifestyle.'

'But how do you know if it's the right person? What about chemistry and the concept of simply falling in love?'

'I've always wondered if love is enough. My parents had lust in the beginning but that didn't last.'

'I doubt anyone would say that a long term commitment in marriage is easy. To give yourself a head start, it seems to me that you need a deep, true love up front. It's hard enough, without starting at a handicap. After that . . . ' she shrugged. 'Who knows what happens in life, and how it changes and turns? Most people seem to compromise and work it out. Isn't that what a life's partnership should be all about?'

She glanced across at Ethan. 'Do you ever visit Meredith in Sydney?'

He shook his head. 'Rarely.'

'Why not?'

'We still keep in touch but we have different lifestyles,' he said wistfully. 'We've just grown apart.'

'It must be hard trying to conduct a relationship long distance. If you care about someone, you want to be with them.'

'Absolutely. Besides, over the last few years, I've come to understand that what I felt for Meredith was probably hormones and youth,' he admitted and fell silent for a moment before adding quietly, 'The chemistry isn't there any more.'

'That's important,' Summer agreed.

'You need that spark.'

The conversation lapsed and they both drifted off into their own thoughts for a while until Ethan reluctantly suggested, 'We should be heading back for those animals before nightfall.'

He stood and held out a hand, pulling her up beside him.

'Thanks for a fabulous meal and the nature lesson,' she quipped, deliberately standing close and not moving away.

When the spark of attraction flared in his eyes and then died, she stepped back and gave a shaky smile to hide her disappointment. If Ethan was choosing a partner based on whether or not she ticked all the appropriate social class boxes, Summer knew she would end up somewhere way down towards the bottom of his list.

The return drive to the Peters' property was completed in silence. Ethan hooked up the trailer and backed the vehicle up to the holding yards. He helped Peter and one of his staff load the three alpacas while she sorted out the pedigree papers with Jenny, and they started the drive home just as it was growing dark.

Summer yawned and settled to contemplate the day's events as the car lights lit a path on the darkening road ahead. Traffic was light and her mind blanked as the miles sped by.

She must have dozed off long before they reached Greenbanks, because she gradually became aware of a familiar deep voice calling her name. Someone was stroking her hair and gently shaking her shoulder then the same voice, very close to her ear, murmured, 'Wake up, Sleeping Beauty. Your hundred years is up.'

Summer woke to see Ethan bending over her in the passenger seat. She stretched and yawned. 'Home already?'

And for the first time realised that this was home now. Still semi-conscious as she struggled to stay awake, she felt herself being scooped up in a powerful pair of arms.

'You're as light as a lamb,' Ethan

murmured against her hair. Summer slid her arms about his neck, still dozy.

After a brief bumpy ride, Ethan put her gently down on her bed. 'I'll lock all your doors when I leave.'

Summer stole a sleepy glance at Ethan and yawned. 'Don't bother. I never do.'

'Even at night?'

She heard the grumpy edge in his voice but was too sleepy to be annoyed and simply shook her head. He gave a sigh of frustration and she snuggled into her pillow, grinning to herself. 'I don't have anything worth stealing,' she argued languidly. 'Besides, I have my neighbour to protect me.'

'I guess I'll take a rain check on that cuppa you promised.'

She felt a tender kiss pressed to her forehead and because she fell asleep again almost instantly, didn't hear Ethan leave.

★   ★   ★

Next morning, Summer sprang up in bed, suddenly remembering last night, arriving home, Ethan carrying her to bed. She knew something was wrong with the picture.

Oh, my God — she forgot to unload the alpacas!

Misty tumbled over on the bed-clothes and onto the floor, mewing with fright as her owner flung aside the covers and scrambled from the house still fully dressed in her jeans and gypsy shirt, but dishevelled and crumpled from sleeping in them all night.

A sprint outside to see what on earth had happened to her precious new arrivals was rewarded with the wonder-ful vision of all three contentedly grazing in the nearest paddock to the cottage. The cream one looked up as she chewed and disinterestedly turned her long neck in Summer's direction. Her body relaxed and she groaned, realising to her shame that Ethan must have unloaded them for her last night.

Filled with gratitude and making a

note to call him later with her thanks, she lingered at the fence, staring at her small starter flock in adoration. Even though the Peters had named them from their own stud, Summer decided to give each animal a name of its own for her property.

Because the cream one seemed so docile she called her Greenbank Serenity. The dusky pregnant female she wasn't sure yet; she would observe her personality and name her later. The wether companion further down the paddock was independently doing its own thing, so she chose Greenbank Gypsy.

'Morning, Laddie.' Summer bent down to pat him as he trotted over from the cottage to see what all the activity and fuss was about.

Misty came bounding across the mown grass, apparently recovered from her unceremonious awakening on the bed.

Summer scooped up the fluffy bundle and murmured an apology.

Just as she was about to head across to the girls in the chook yard and gather the eggs, Ethan arrived. He was getting to be a regular fixture around the place.

'Morning,' he greeted, striding toward her, full of energy and exciting male charisma, looking fresh and handsome in beige moleskins with a black tee shirt topped by his trademark big black hat.

'I can make you that cuppa now I'm awake,' she grinned.

'When you sleep, you sure make a proper job of it.' He leaned over the fence beside her.

'I think getting the place established over the past weeks finally caught up with me.'

'You should take more time off.'

'Yesterday was . . . wonderful,' she murmured.

'Sure was,' he agreed softly.

'Thanks for helping me last night — and for unloading the animals. I normally have much more stamina.'

'Any time.'

Since it was still early and she was

starving, Summer asked, 'Have you had breakfast yet?'

'Nope.'

'Interested?'

'Why do you think I came over? You're such a great cook.'

She took a deep breath and stepped back, overwhelmed by his dangerous smile. 'Come on up to the house, then. But give me a minute to get the wood fire going and change my clothes.'

Half an hour later, flames licked around the kindling in the firebox, the kettle was singing and Summer had reappeared in black leggings and a long floppy shirt. She had run a brush through her hair but left it hanging long and loose.

Ethan's hungry gaze settled on her as she strolled back into the kitchen, making her unexpectedly selfconscious, but she determined not to read too much into it.

Meanwhile, she intended to play it cautious. She wasn't the only person to consider, if and when she ever formed another relationship with a man who became important in her life. She had a daughter — whose emotional stability was always Summer's primary concern.

Ivy had never known the constancy of a father figure in her life, apart from a reasonably regular association with her grandfather.

Shaking off her thoughts, Summer ripped a handful of herbs from among the jungle of greenery growing in the row of small terracotta pots along the deep windowsill. 'If you could get eggs, milk and bacon out of the fridge, I can make a start,' she said brightly. She sliced thick slabs of her homemade rye bread and set them aside, then gathered an earthenware bowl and whisk to make a start on their breakfast.

'What's this?' Ethan's brow wrinkled in amusement as he held up the fresh eggs from her girls, on which she occasionally painted funny faces.

She looked up from chopping parsley and chives, and laughed. 'Oops. Caught,' she shrugged off her silly habit, adding,

'Cute, aren't they?'

'Certainly original.'

He perched on the edge of the table juggling two eggs. 'Careful with those,' she teased as she laid strips of bacon in a pan to spit and sizzle. 'My girls worked hard to produce them.'

'They look like little people without legs.' He shook his head in amused disbelief.

'Well, theoretically, they are,' she pointed out, playing along. She'd never seen Ethan so relaxed nor in such good humour. When they first met, he was dour and serious but he had lightened up considerably in the weeks since then. Being neighbours and flung into regular contact, they'd begun to know and understand each other better.

The egg liquid hissed as Summer poured it into another pan and lightly turned the mixture until it was softly set. She spooned out the eggs onto plates, draped the crispy bacon on top and tucked the slices of chunky bread on the side.

'You didn't really come over here just for breakfast, did you?' Summer queried as they ate companionably together at the kitchen table.

'It was in the back of my mind,' he admitted, 'But actually I forgot to mention yesterday about the annual fête coming up that we hold over at the homestead. With your cooking and craft ability, I thought you might like to be on the organising committee.'

'Jean Miller mentioned the CWA have a tent to sell their produce and raise funds. What exactly does this committee do?'

'Basically organise everything for the day. Jean's on the committee too. The CWA ladies do all the catering. It's a big event and we get hundreds of visitors. The first committee meeting is over at Karingal Park next Wednesday.'

Summer made a wry face. 'Oh, all right. I don't usually do committees. I hate all that taking of minutes and red tape, but since you asked so nicely and it's to support local worthy causes, I'll come. Will you be there among all the ladies and cups of tea?'

'I usually put in an appearance.' He grinned.

9

Three days later, Summer's slim shoulders drooped in despair. Would they care what she wore? More to the point, did she? But the thought of encountering Victoria Bourke again left her reassessing her appearance. It wasn't her intention to try to impress her — simply not to embarrass herself.

Despondently, she eyed the contents of her wardrobe. She'd only brought work clothes and nothing remotely dressy . . . well, she had tossed in one little number, although she'd never worn it. A simple cream cotton maxi dress she'd bought from the charity shop and made over with touches of cheap but pretty lace.

She slipped it on and wriggled into it. Her now tanned skin showed up against the pale fabric as she added an antique second-hand bracelet she had swapped at a market recently for a dozen eggs.

Lavender was her favourite flower this time of year with its strong fragrance soaking the air so she snipped a sprig from a bush in her garden and caught it up into one side of her hair with a plain clip holding it away from her face.

As Summer pulled up on the crunchy gravel at the front of Karingal Park homestead later, she was relieved to see Jean Miller just arriving, heading briskly for the wide bluestone steps.

Jean turned at the familar sound of the noisy vehicle approaching behind her and waved, waiting for Summer to catch up. 'Good to see you here,' she greeted her warmly, smiling. 'We need more young blood.'

'Ethan asked if I would be interested.'

'Good for him,' Jean said enthusiastically. 'Always have the same people year after year and we get in a rut. We need fresh ideas if we want to keep drawing the crowds.' She pressed the bell and they heard its echo from somewhere distant in the house.

A thin, middle-aged woman in a stylish floral dress opened the mammoth cedar front door, filled with two long panels of stained glass.

'Afternoon, Audrey.' Jean bustled in without ado and introduced Summer. 'In the drawing room?'

Audrey nodded and smiled warmly. 'You know your way. I'll get back to the kitchen.'

When she disappeared and they crossed the black and white tiled floor of the entry hall, Jean leaned closer and hissed, 'Spinster. Family had a large grazing property but it was divided up among the sons and their wealth dwindled. She lives in a townhouse in Hamilton now, but helps out here when needed. Brilliant cook. Even though Audrey's come down a bit in her generation, she's a lovely lady and Victoria considers she's still the same social class and therefore acceptable.'

'Really?' Summer wasn't fully concentrating. She was gaping at the impressive chandelier dripping with crystal, its candleholders converted to electric globes. She followed Jean along the hall beside a massive cedar staircase until they entered a plush, grand room already half filled with ladies and impressive with velvet drapes and deep fabric sofas. A white marble fireplace with gilt mirror above was graced by an enormous bowl of white roses.

Summer was struck by the affluence, although inherited from a bygone era and enjoyed by its current occupants. Ethan had been right. This was meant to be a family home. Somehow, despite its grandeur, its potential was lost and it felt empty and sad.

Her awe was swiftly diverted by Victoria and an elegant dark-haired woman seated beside her in crisp slacks, tailored white shirt and pearls. Summer felt positively rustic, regardless of the effort she had made, and sighed that she had no better footwear than sandals.

She smiled and greeted Victoria,

receiving only mock charm and a synthetic smile in response. When Jean introduced the younger, confident woman, she was proved right. It couldn't have been anyone other than Meredith Wells.

'Summer! Welcome to the district,' the tall woman gushed graciously, as though she still lived here and had the authority to speak on behalf of the locals. Being born in the district, perhaps she still did. Her acknowledgement was fleeting and indifferent but at least appeared more genuine than the hostess's.

With the arrival of the last few women and everyone comfortable in plush chairs and sofas, the meeting started, with Victoria taking control.

She played the lady of the manor with aplomb but it wasn't hard to spot the odd slip, loud word or proud empty laugh. Summer stared at her in amazement. She was half tipsy! Meredith, sitting on Victoria's right, steered her back on track if she faltered. Which was often.

Victoria took every opportunity to

challenge or override suggestions. She rudely cut in on the middle of discussions, and generally flaunted her superiority, always needing the last say in decisions.

Perhaps living in a big house and coming from wealthy ancestors had given her an exaggerated sense of self-importance. If she had much more to do with this woman, Summer felt she wouldn't be able to hold her tongue. She wondered why the local women all simply sat there, charitably enduring this bossy woman.

Tolerant glances passed between the women as discussions progressed about who was organising what, who was responsible for what, and who was bringing what. All necessary, Summer was sure, but she grew restless and bored even over the details to be sorted.

Then mercifully, it wound up. Notepads were stuffed in handbags, a general air of relief and ease filled the staunch group and Audrey shuffled in and out with plates of lavish food and trays of cups and saucers.

Victoria and Meredith sat apart, making no effort to socialise with the other women. Summer wondered if the younger woman was being tactful, since Victoria's face was flushed and she looked confused.

Without warning above the conversation and from across the room, Victoria suddenly rallied and her crisp loud voice carried to everyone. 'Tell me, Miss Dalton, how are your parents? Did they every marry?'

Summer ignored the last barb because she felt certain it was common knowledge they weren't. But she was stung and angry at the deliberate public attack. Must be a dose of Dutch courage from the drink.

'They're both well. Thank you for asking,' she responded calmly.

'Do they still live in a sort of . . . what is it? A commune?' Victoria's mouth pulled into a distasteful twist.

Summer clamped down on a biting retort and took a deep breath before responding. 'Yes, they do — and they love it there.'

She noticed some of the women squirming in their seats at the loaded exchange until their attention was distracted. Summer followed their gazes across the room to see Ethan standing silently in the doorway with a thunderous scowl on his face.

When he strolled forward, relaxed and gorgeous in moleskins and a black and grey checked shirt, it wasn't only Summer's heart that melted. Every woman gave a silent collective sigh and gazed at him as though he were bush royalty.

He ignored his mother and Meredith, working the room, individually acknowledging each woman present, sparing a brief personal word, asking after family or children.

Before reaching the end of the guest circle, Ethan flashed a glance in Summer's direction then pointedly turned to his mother with a glacial stare. 'Mother, can I have a word?'

Victoria smiled stiffly and paled. She looked like a peeved child forced to do as she was told against her will. Summer felt awkward on Ethan's behalf and compassion for his damaged mother. After an agitated moment, Meredith rose and followed. What a scandal!

Over distant muffled voices, the drawing room occupants relaxed.

'Are they always like this?' Summer leaned over to ask Jean.

The older woman chuckled, keeping her voice low. 'Victoria is notorious for a bit of drama. Don't take it too seriously. It's kind of a ritual the first time anyone comes to visit. Gives us all a bit of a giggle.'

Coming from a community where every man, woman and child had an equal standing and voice, Summer was appalled.

'I'm surprised you tolerate it. Surely you all have more self-respect and consideration than to let someone be so spiteful?'

Conversations stopped and heads turned. Jean's startled gaze told her she had crossed a line. Maybe she had, and this small, insulated community was prepared to accept the status quo — but Summer could hold no admiration for Victoria Bourke. She had had every privilege in her life yet was miserable and inflicting that bitter unhappiness on everyone around her. The woman was crying out for help. She wondered who would dare to offer it before she self-destructed.

A cold, uneasy silence blanketed the room. When Victoria, Meredith and Ethan reappeared as if nothing had happened, Summer politely endured the afternoon tea, planning to leave as soon as possible.

* * *

Ethan stayed in the background in the drawing room among the ladies with a delicate cup of tea perched on his knee while he ate one of Audrey's savouries, keeping an eye on his mother after her unforgivable outburst. And also to watch Summer, who had borne the onslaught with her usual quiet grace.

Settled so easily into an armchair like a part of the house, Summer lit up the room. Today, in her light coloured dress with a rich tan, she glowed. Despite her simplicity — or perhaps because of it — she stood out, possessed of a beauty beyond the senses, a lithe and natural unforced elegance. He believed she had no idea how she could draw the breath out of a man's chest.

Whereas Meredith possessed a classically cultivated beauty gifted to her from a privileged education and with the benefit of expensive clothes, Summer's appeal came from her inner beauty and emotional poise — neither of which could be bought with money.

Bitten by a sudden restless energy, Ethan finally admitted what he had known for a long time. Karingal Park didn't need any more thoroughbreds. It needed a woman of character who would make this mausoleum a home again.

'Ethan!' Victoria snapped.

His mother's sharp voice refocused his attention in her direction.

'The telephone,' she admonished crisply.

With a half wave and rueful smile at his distraction, but secretly pleased to escape, an amused grin spread across his face as he walked down the hall, chuckling over Summer's feet. He was willing to bet anything that Victoria's eyes had popped over the butterfly anklet and purple painted toenails.

After the phone call, Ethan didn't return to the drawing room but loitered on the front steps, playing with Brewster. Waiting.

When the object of his patience appeared as one of the first to leave, Ethan rose and grabbed her elbow. 'Come with me.'

Amused, Summer gently wrenched it away. 'You're just as bossy as your mother, you know.'

Ethan flashed a devastating smile that would crumble the strongest defences. 'Irresistible, aren't we?'

'I couldn't answer that with a civil tongue.'

He placed a prompting hand gently at her waist and pleaded, 'Let's walk together.'

With an overplayed sigh of indulgence, Summer nodded and they headed off across the vast lawns leading away from the house and down a slight rise toward a pond.

'You were very gracious under fire,' he remarked as they sat on a stone seat at the water's edge.

'Yes, you must thank your mother for her attempted hospitality,' Summer returned with impish spirit.

'I overheard. I don't believe she realised she embarrassed herself more than anyone else.' He bent forward and looked down at the grass, hands folded on his knees and Summer sensed his confusion.

She shrugged, enjoying the private moment with him if not the topic of conversation. 'Everyone has a good and bad side,' she said generously.

'I apologise for her,' he said gently.

'Isn't that her responsibility?'

'Probably.'

'Her actions are not your fault, but I understand you might feel blame by association. You mentioned she was insecure and unhappy, but I had no idea how much. I feel sorry for her.'

Ethan scowled in frustration. 'I've tried to suggest she should get help but she won't have it.'

'I appreciate your honesty. She does need urgent help, Ethan.'

'You're not telling me something I don't already know,' he agreed, doggedly rubbing a hand across his brow in frustration. 'You can lead a horse to water, Summer . . . '

A breeze drifted past, rustling the willow leaves by the lake. Birds twittered somewhere up high among leafy summer branches.

'Meredith's lovely,' Summer said after a while when it seemed the topic of his mother was done.

He sighed. 'Unfortunately she indulges Victoria, which is why they get on so well. But it doesn't help Mother.'

Brewster wandered up to them and sat down nearby, panting. Summer reached out and fondled his ears. 'Is Meredith staying long?'

He shrugged. 'No idea. She doesn't like the country any more, so I guess not. I gained the impression she still wants us to be together — but on her terms.'

'Do *you?*' Summer squinted across the lake glistening with diamonds of sunlight, hanging on his answer yet not sure if she wanted to hear it.

Ethan rose, and turned to face her, sinking his hands into his pockets and placing one booted foot up on the stone seat beside her. He shook his head. 'We had the big talk last night. Meredith came over for dinner and Mother tactfully left us alone. It was hard, but I told her that I saw no future together for us.'

'I'm sorry. That can't have been easy.'

'It wasn't, but Meredith's wrapped up in herself and her city life.' He grimaced. 'She actually expected me to put a manager on the property and go to live in Sydney.'

'You could never do that! You'd wither.'

Ethan cast Summer a long, strange look of contemplation. 'Yes, you're right, I would. But how do you know that after a matter of weeks when Meredith has never realised it?'

She gave a soft smile. 'I watch people. I've learned to listen.'

He reached out and caught her hands, drawing her up in front of him, very close. Still holding her hands, he murmured, 'How is your girl?'

Summer never thought she could feel such a heady sense of joy from the pleasure of someone else's company. Usually not one to deny her feelings, she took a deep breath to fight it. 'Which one?' she teased, feeling breathless. 'Ivy, the chooks or the alpacas?'

'The pregnant female alpaca,' he said with deliberate tolerance.

'I know that's what you meant,' she admitted, smiling. 'I'm keeping an eye on her.'

It seemed the most natural gesture in the world that he should put a hand at the back of her waist and draw her that bit closer. She knew she was about to be kissed, wanted to be and would revel in it. But when his lips actually touched hers, it lit a fiery response from deep within that completely overwhelmed her.

She moaned when it ended, shaken, as he whispered, 'I've been wanting to do that for a while.'

'It was worth the wait.'

'Pleased to hear it.' He kissed her again, long and tenderly. Crushed against him, with her arms around his neck, Summer knew there was no place else in the world she would rather be.

'Ethan?'

At the sound of Meredith calling out his name across the lawns from the homestead, he broke away from Summer and cursed. Running an impatient hand through his hair, he grinned and took her hand.

'Back to civilisation,' he said, adding softly, 'To be continued . . . '

'Promises, promises,' she chuckled.

The comprehensive killer glare that Meredith blazed over them as they trudged back up the hill together and approached the house holding hands, might have deterred lesser spirits and spoken volumes.

Ethan merely flashed an easy genuine smile, as though he walked up from the lake holding a woman's hand every day.

Summer, now she knew that he shared her feelings, was acutely aware that seeing Ethan with another woman must sting Meredith. Especially since he had only just ended their relationship.

Gracious in loss, once Meredith had her emotions under control, her shocked chilly stare was swiftly replaced by a pleasant, cool smile.

'I thought everyone had left,' she said unnecessarily.

'Obviously not,' Ethan answered. 'Are you leaving?'

'No. I'm not.'

'Did someone want me?'

'Your mother . . . ' Meredith gestured vaguely toward the house.

'What now?' Ethan muttered and released Summer's hand to bound up the broad front steps two at a time. He glanced back at Summer with hopeful raised eyebrows.

With a slight shake of her head sending her lovely long hair rustling around her shoulders, she said, 'I'll be off. Nice to meet you, Meredith.'

When her warm smile was not acknowledged in any way by the other woman, she said softly, 'Peace,' and left.

Before she reached the van, she heard Meredith's sibilant voice drift clearly down from the veranda in disapproval. 'Honestly, Ethan, do you know what you're doing with that girl?'

As she drove away, Summer silently

absorbed the pain of Meredith's cutting remark, a cruel dampener from the high after she and Ethan had kissed. She wished she'd heard his response.

She gripped the steering wheel and groaned. She should be bubbling with happiness, but instead their lovely memorable moment in the garden had been tainted.

All the same, before she considered her swelling feelings and any relationship with Ethan, it forced her to re-evaluate their differences — his mother with her problems and non-acceptance . . . Ivy . . . Summer came with extras, and their backgrounds couldn't be further apart.

Were there too many hurdles to overcome? Summer usually confronted each day as it arrived but with her deep feelings for Ethan, transforming into emotions impossible to deny, she had so much to lose if anything went wrong.

10

Ethan found he couldn't stay away from Greenbanks and its new owner for long. This morning as he turned in at the gate — that still needed replacing, he noticed — he had a specific mission in mind. To address Meredith's brutal words that Summer must surely have overheard. He bit back a silent curse, wishing his mother and Meredith would keep their unjustified criticisms of Summer to themselves. After the tragedy and loneliness his family has weathered, he had hoped they might at least be happy for him. No such luck.

Meredith had been verbally stripping. Her prejudice and intolerance showed her up in a new and unflattering light. It only confirmed in his mind that he had made the right decision to end their association.

Disappointed not to find Summer in

her cottage and knowing the cria's birth was imminent, he wandered down to the nearest paddock where she kept the animals until after the big event.

He caught sight of her sitting on the grass under a shady tree, arms outstretched and resting loosely on her knees, legs crossed, slender back straight. He couldn't see but presumed her eyes were closed and she was engrossed in some kind of meditation. He marvelled at her stillness. It reminded him of Brewster when he lifted a front paw and froze like a statue while herding sheep; relaxed but alert.

From beneath the undulating brim of her black felt hat, strands of her long hair teased away from her shoulders by a playful breeze. He hesitated to approach and disturb her, wondering at her ability for such tranquillity and ease of mind in the wake of Meredith's nasty words yesterday. He admired the fact that such a feminine soul possessed an inner strength and tenacity.

At first he'd been fuelled by an unfair

bias because of her unorthodox appearance. He regretted his misjudgement. Now, he adored her.

Gripped by a fierce attraction, he worried that because of their different lives, an issue that seemed to bother Summer but which didn't concern him at all, she might not consider him as more than a neighbour and a friend. Although she had readily returned his kiss, and that gave him hope.

When he stepped forward, she moved slightly. Perhaps sensing his approach, she turned and gifted him with a serene smile of welcome.

'Sorry.' He paused. 'Didn't mean to interrupt you.'

'I've been aware of you for some time.' She patted the grass beside her and he hunkered down to settle his large frame alongside. 'I'm paddock watching.'

'I can see that.' He chuckled, finding it frustrating wanting to touch her but unsure after his family's poor performance if it would be welcomed.

'Serenity hasn't been as interested in grazing lately and there's a definite drop in her belly. Could be a sign of early labour — not today but close, perhaps tomorrow. I phoned Jenny Peters this morning, and she's as thrilled as me. It's like having your own child. Scary, but exciting.'

Unable to withstand her appeal any longer, Ethan murmured, 'Can I distract you and steal a kiss, then?'

She sighed and a lurking grin tilted her tempting mouth. 'Ethan Bourke. Sometimes you're too much the gentleman. Stealing suggests taking without permission.'

She turned toward him, bringing their faces close, shoulders touching. A faint and familiar drift of lavender flowed about her.

'In future,' she whispered, 'because I return your feelings, consider you have my permission to give me all manner of kisses and affection.'

He took immediate advantage of her offer.

When their deep, lingering kiss ended, Summer breathed, 'Amazing.'

They shared a secret smile, childish in their discovery of each other.

'I couldn't agree more.'

'Do you know, that when two planets are aligned, their energy intensifies and focuses?'

'You're not kidding. Ours must be well and truly in sync then.'

Summer threw back her head and laughed, a magical gift of sound that Ethan quietly absorbed and used to slowly heal his wounded soul. He shared her laughter until they both fell back onto the grass holding hands. Summer's hat tumbled off onto the ground.

They stared up into the tree above where sun drops tried to sparkle through the gaps between the leaves, revelling together in the joy of new-found romance.

When their exhilaration faded, Ethan said softly, 'I'm sorry, if you overheard Meredith yesterday.'

Summer turned aside to look at him, then rolled over to prop herself up on one elbow. 'No drama. I know they don't approve of me. I don't fit the image, or the acceptable mould, to be your lady friend. They're afraid of what they don't know.'

'But you're not, are you? You embrace truth and knowledge. You're a plucky soul and, as good fortune would have it,' Ethan sat up and reached for her hand, 'I'm beginning to care for you very much.'

Summer squinted and looked past his shoulder across the paddock to the alpacas, recovering her hat and patting it back onto her head. 'Oh, Ethan,' she confessed with a weary sigh. 'I'm not sure you should.'

'I have no doubts. This is about you and me. No one else.'

'I know, but . . . '

'But what?'

'I'm bound to shock and embarrass you. You spring from a family with such traditional establishment values, I'm not sure I'd fit in. I tend to push boundaries.' She paused. 'Could you cope with that?' she asked softly.

'I have done so far.'

'You do understand what I'm saying?'

'Sure. You're not as radical as you think. I care about the land, the earth, and the planet, too. I want exactly the same things you do. A deeply loving and lasting partnership with someone for life. I'd be in it for the long haul. Prepared to make it work. Forever.'

Summer flashed him a cheeky smile. 'You're quite a man.'

'You're pretty special yourself.' Ethan leaned over and kissed her again before he rose reluctantly. 'I have to meet Jack, then make a trip into Hamilton. I'll catch you later and see how things are progressing.'

'There'll probably be no action until early morning,' Summer said. She watched him stride away, strong, handsome, distinguished. Filled with growing joy and hope.

She had fallen for Billy quickly, too,

but it was nothing compared to this because it hadn't been true love. Now she knew the difference and shook her head, astounded that it should be with the man climbing the rise back toward the cottage.

She hugged her knees and smiled, pleading with whatever deity was out there, clinging to the dream that this blossoming romance promising so much healing and freedom for them both would develop all the way. Her bubbly heart billowed at the prospect.

Because Serenity had joined the small herd again to feed in the paddock, Summer took a break from watching, hoping that nothing happened while she was away.

She hadn't seen Enid since she had moved into care in Hamilton, so she decided to make a quick trip into town with Laddie to the hostel and visit the gracious elderly lady. Her new home must be strange, and it would take time to readjust. Seeing a familiar friend might cheer her up if she was feeling lost.

Before she left, Summer phoned Jean

for her son's contact number. Amazingly, her busy friend was home so she immediately phoned Sean and he arranged to meet her late in the day to organise cutting her hay.

As she had suspected, Enid was delighted to see Laddie. They sat out in the courtyard garden under the trees and chatted while Enid glowed with happiness, her sheltie devotedly close alongside.

* * *

At length, Summer rattled toward home in her van, elated. Ethan cared about her. Enid was quietly settling into her new life. Her alpacas were about to increase by one. Ivy would be with her soon. She felt as if her life could not be any better.

She recognised Julie Williams' car approaching, heading into town. They tooted and waved to each other as they passed.

'Oh, Laddie, life's enough of a high

without needing any artificial stimulants, huh?'

In her rear view mirror, she smiled at the dog securely leashed in the back of the vehicle. He gave a quick yap as if he understood.

When Sean Miller pulled up in her yard later and emerged from his throaty farm Ute with a forest of radio antennae wavering from its roof and towing a hay baler, Summer instantly recognised him. How could she not, with his trademark Miller red hair and freckles?

'Summer.' He greeted her warmly, shaking hands.

He had the same lovely round face as his mother, not to mention her vivacious energy. Having refreshed him with a large glass of cold homemade lemonade, she led the way to the machinery shed, checking out and admiring her alpacas on the way.

'Serenity's about to give birth any day. I'm getting anxious.'

'Well, let's take your mind off it. I can

make a start on the hay today.' He squinted toward the lower paddocks near the dam. 'Weather's coming, so it's best to get it off as soon as possible. Under this sun, it'll certainly be dry enough.'

He hung over the tractor engine, checking the oil and water, explaining so Summer could do it herself next time. She had never used machinery before, so this was all a new experience. Like most farmers, Amos had left the key in the ignition so Sean turned it over and after a couple of splutters, it kicked into life.

'Sure makes a noise!' Summer yelled above the sound.

'I'm surprised it started. It's been sitting in the shed for months. Before I get to work, do you want to take a run around the paddock and I'll give you a driving lesson?'

Summer beamed. 'Unreal! You serious?'

He nodded, amused at her excitement. She needed no urging and he helped her up beside him into the small, cramped cabin. Sean drove it from the shed to the paddock then explained the gears before she took the controls. He stood up, letting her ease in behind the wheel, giving directions and encouragement while she practised.

Summer laughed with exhilaration as they jaunted around the perimeter fence, gaining confidence, although they hardly broke any speed records. The ride was a huge buzz but Sean assured her she was actually quite competent and could drive on her own if she was careful.

'I can't wait to give my daughter a ride in it soon.' Summer steered the tractor back toward the shed so Sean could hook up the baler and get to work on mowing the hay.

'Hope I don't disturb your alpacas.'

'You'll be working in the lower paddocks and some distance away. It shouldn't bother them.'

Sean worked at slashing and piling the hay into windrows until dusk. He had his own food box and water cooler so Summer left him to continue and returned to paddock watching again.

By evening, she was pleasantly weary from a busy day. She called her mother and shared an animated conversation with Ivy about tractor rides and baby alpacas.

After dark, she wandered down to the animals and nervously paced. 'I have no idea what I'm doing out here, Laddie.' She patted the faithful animal, never far from her side. 'Nothing should happen until tomorrow.'

Eventually she conceded and walked back up to the house, but sleep proved elusive. She caught snatches of rest but, just before sunrise, she gave up, made herself a flask of tea, bundled up a rug under her other arm and headed outdoors.

The first streaks of pastel pink and gold light etched themselves across the grey, pre-dawn sky. Never ceasing to be amazed at Nature's beauty, Summer paused to appreciate it for a moment.

Down in the paddock, Serenity had separated herself from the herd, looking restless and uncomfortable. Summer suppressed a squeal of delight. It would be today, after all! She felt as elated as if she was about to give birth herself.

Settling just inside the paddock fence, backed up against a post, she wrapped the blanket around herself. Misty arrived on her early morning explorations, stretched out her front paws, yawned, then curled up in a ball against Summer's legs.

It was in this position that Ethan found them a short while later. Unusually, he was hatless — probably because it was so early, before the day's heat intensified, Summer guessed. Light stubble on his chin suggested he either hadn't bothered to shave or left home in a rush. The golden glow of daybreak played across his thick sandy hair.

He sat beside her and took the liberty of a decent long kiss.

'You're learning,' she teased.

'No, I'm just more sure of you now

we seem to be on the same page.'

'It's scary to risk your emotions.'

'Not any more,' he murmured and kissed her again.

'If you keep this up, I'll miss the birth.'

As Serenity walked about and cushed back down again on the grass beneath a broad old eucalypt, Ethan seemed equally entranced by the birthing process.

'I guess you've seen your share of lambs being born,' Summer said.

'It never loses its pull, though.'

'I've seen plenty of chickens hatch, but Serenity feels part of my family already and her offspring will be as special as Ivy. Oh — look!'

Summer sat forward with eagerness as Serenity began gently rocking from side to side. Needing to be closer, she scrambled to her feet and sauntered further down the paddock. Ethan followed and crouched down beside her. She wished Ivy could witness the miracle of a birth with her, but Ethan

213

was here. His presence revealed the same devotion that stirred in her own heart; an unspoken need to be together.

He reached for her hand and linked fingers. When he leaned closer and his eyes glinted with devilment, she warned, 'Don't you dare distract me. I don't intend to miss any of this.'

They returned their attention to the expectant mother who had raised her tail and started to push. The cria's face emerged first.

'No feet yet,' Summer whispered. Then the membrane broke and legs plopped out. As she held her breath, the baby instinctively wriggled and rumbled until it was fully free.

'Congratulations,' Ethan said as they beamed at each other.

It took a while for the scraggly cream cria and its mother to recover. They waited patiently until, almost an hour later, the newborn struggled to its feet and took its first tottering steps.

'Her face is so sweet,' Summer said. 'I'll call her Tinkerbell.'

Ethan grinned. 'Suits her.'

'Nature never ceases to amaze, does it? Jenny told me the cria would be born early in the day because it has time to gain strength, dry off and start drinking from its mother before dark.'

'Lambs aren't that considerate,' Ethan moaned. 'I often do a midnight paddock run in the autumn around my stud ewes.'

'Poor Ethan. You'll just have to start breeding alpacas and make your life so much easier,' she teased, still euphoric over Tinkerbell's birth.

'We need to celebrate,' Ethan suggested.

'I don't keep alcohol but I have chilled lemonade,' she told him.

'Don't suppose you'd do breakfast again?'

Summer nudged him playfully as they eventually tore themselves away from the paddock and ambled back up to the house. 'Well, my first birth is over. All I need now is to get my animals shorn.'

'I offered to do that, remember?'

'So you did. Oh, I forgot in this morning's excitement — Sean Miller taught me how to drive my tractor yesterday,' she announced with pride. 'So,' she added, filled with mischief, 'If Blossom breaks down, I can use it in an emergency to come and see you.'

Ethan shook his head. 'Romantic way of dating.'

'Are we?' Summer queried softly.

'I reckon we've made a start.' He flung an affectionate arm around her shoulder. 'But I can do flowers and chocolates, too, if you like.'

'Not necessary. You can shear my alpacas instead. I'm sure they'll appreciate the relief now that warmer weather is in the air.'

'Feed me another of your famous breakfasts and I'm all yours.'

'Actually — ' she squinted at the sky. 'It's probably more like brunch.'

'I'll need to check my diary, but will later in the week be okay for shearing? Shouldn't take more than an hour or two for all three animals.'

While indulging themselves over a leisurely meal of herb and bacon omelettes, Summer asked, 'Does Victoria know how often you visit?' She was concerned about the animosity their relationship might create.

He shook his head. 'I come and go as I please. I don't answer to anyone, but she was still in bed when I left. She's not a morning person. You're worried,' he said gently.

'Of course. I'd be the last person on your mother's dinner guest list.'

'Ah.' Ethan flashed one of his knee-buckling devastating grins. 'But I can invite people, too. Don't fret.' He grew serious again. 'Life has a way of resolving issues.'

'That sounds like something I would say. And you're right, of course; brooding solves nothing.'

After Ethan left and because she knew Ivy would be rapt to have the same experience, Summer phoned Julie Williams for the telephone number of the small local primary school. Around

217

midday, when she thought it might be most convenient, she called, receiving an ecstatic response to her proposition.

'Summer, that's a fabulous idea,' Sandra Bailey, the teacher, said. 'The children often see lambs but a baby alpaca will be fascinating. We often have field trips on a Friday. Is this week too soon?'

Summer assured her it was not, so they scheduled an excursion and Summer planned special baked treats plus free rein in the orchard and among her girls clucking about in the yard. Most of the children lived on farms and realised where their food came from, but she hoped all the activities would prove stimulating — they could fossick for their own fruit, eggs and herbs to take home.

As it happened, Ethan phoned back to confirm he could shear the alpacas on the same day.

'Far out.' Summer laughed. 'This outing might become the highlight of the semester for the children.'

11

On the day, Summer rose early to prepare batches of peach muffins. She had bought brown paper bags on which the children could write their names to take home the morning's goodies. When the school mini bus arrived, the students tumbled out, exuberant and loud.

'Pleased to escape the classroom,' Sandra explained, coming forward to introduce herself.

Like a pied piper, the children followed Summer as she led them all down to the alpaca paddock, announcing the extra treats of shearing and a garden excursion before they returned to school.

Chattering with excitement, they took turns in small groups in the paddock, leading the haltered alpacas, learning about them and spoiling

Tinkerbell — the highlight of their visit.

Summer missed Ethan's arrival until, amid the chaos, she prickled with an awareness that drew her attention toward the fence. He was watching her, surrounded by children, unmistakable admiration in his eyes.

A glow spread through her at the sight of him and she waved. He returned the gesture and threw in a killer smile. He was so damned gorgeous, she wanted to leap the fence and plant a serious kiss on those generous lips. Sandra sidled up to him and Summer surged with jealousy. *Foolish woman*, she berated herself. *They know each other. It's harmless.* But it didn't help, knowing that Sandra was single.

The shearing activity drew half the children's group at a time and shook Summer's peace of mind even more. She helped Ethan to get each alpaca lying down and tied their front and back sets of legs together. Working close, she found it a challenge to keep her mind off his athletically muscled body, rugged in a black singlet and gleaming with perspiration as he worked.

As he ran the clippers through the fabulous fleece, Summer noted he took particular care with Serenity. His big hands were skilled and gentle but the children's fascinated questions helped keep her focused.

'Does it hurt Gypsy to be tied up?'

'No.' Summer put a reassuring arm around the girl's shoulder. 'She looks awkward but she's quite comfortable.'

'Will Tinkerbell be shorn?' a boy asked.

'No, not yet, she's too young. Maybe next year when she's bigger.'

'Why is Gypsy lying down?'

'It's easier for her and less stressful. Mr Bourke only takes about ten minutes to shear each one so they're not in that position for long.'

Mr Bourke, sweaty but handsome, was proving a stirring distraction.

With a twisted sense of relief, Summer took half the children who had seen the shearing off to visit the poultry. 'This speckled one is Anastasia. The two white ones are Dominica and Isabella.'

'Who's your favourite?' a child asked.

Summer didn't hesitate. 'Henrietta. The brown one.'

She had deliberately not fed her girls yet this morning so, while some of the children scattered feed pellets and kitchen scraps in the yard, the others gathered eggs from the straw-filled laying boxes.

'They're still warm,' one girl said with delight.

'Can't get fresher than that, can you?' Summer laughed.

The orchard proved an equal treat and baskets were soon crammed with citrus fruit and peaches. When everyone gathered back up at the house, some of the older children chosen by Sandra sorted and counted the produce and filled the bags.

With a sense of exhausted fulfilment, Summer waved them goodbye as the minibus disappeared down the lane back to the main road, trailing the usual cloud of dust. In a quiet word to Sandra before they left, she had arranged to meet the teacher after school one day soon and enrol Ivy in a year's time.

Summer drank in an eyeful of Ethan striding up to the house.

'That went well.' He grinned. 'They'll be talking about it for weeks.'

'Thanks for the special shearing exhibition.'

He would never know how much she had appreciated him — in more ways than one. She silently groaned with pleasure when he peeled off his singlet and sluiced his body in cool water at the laundry sink. Arms folded, leaning against the door, gawping, Summer heaved a long contented sigh of yearning at his wickedly packed torso.

'I have a chicken curry simmering. Stay for lunch?'

He glanced aside as he towelled himself dry. 'Need you ask? The way to a man's heart, you know . . . '

'Is that the only reason you visit?'

'Oh, I can think of others.'

He held her gaze and heat scooted through her body at his blatant study of appreciation. He had no need to touch her to make her feel adored. She hid amusement when he appeared in the kitchen a short time later, hair damp and shirt open, smelling of lavender. He had used her body lotion to freshen up!

Summer spooned her creamy chicken curry and steamed rice into deep bowls. They took them and a dish of chapattis out onto the front porch seat, eating in companionable silence for a while, observing the newly shorn alpacas foraging contentedly in the home paddock.

'You know, I believe you were born to love,' Ethan said casually, loading a mouthful of curry onto a piece of the flat bread.

Summer stilled. 'Was I?' How had he so easily advanced from being a man who kept her wary with reservation to someone she craved so?

'You were so warm and generous with the children this morning. You gave a lot of thought and preparation to their visit.'

Summer shrugged. 'They're easy to love.'

'Not for everyone.'

He set down his empty bowl and became thoughtful, squinting off into the distance, away across the hills. Was he thinking of his mother? She empathised with his dilemma and considered anew the thorny implications of her potentially deeper involvement with the Bourke family through him.

Before she had a chance to comment, Ethan said, 'Simon and I were raised with a succession of nannies. We gave 'em hell but as soon as we were old enough, it was off to private boarding school. I appreciate that we had a privileged education, but no child of mine will ever endure the misery of separation from his parents and home,' he said fiercely, adding on a more philosophical note, 'I only ever wanted to stay on the

225

farm and bus into the local school.'

'I agree. Families take all shapes but if it's possible, growing up in a close and loving family unit is the ideal. It doesn't always happen though.' She flashed him an ironic smile.

'Parents don't get a manual. They do the best they can with who they are. We can't go back, but each generation can learn from the past and decide for themselves if they want to do things differently.'

He turned and let his mouth twitch into a wry grin. 'Am I getting too serious now?'

Summer chuckled. 'You're a deep thinker. When I first met you, I mistook it for snobbery.'

'Glad you worked that one out.' He reached out for her and drew her up beside him.

'Time to get back to work,' he groaned some time later. 'You're becoming a major distraction, Ms Dalton.'

He slid his arms about her waist once

more and she responded eagerly to his kissing. Snuggled against him, Summer rested her head against his shoulder, savouring his warmth and company. She was almost tempted to plunge in and blurt out her feelings there and then, but something held her back, not yet ready to make that leap.

She needed to give herself more time. Wait until Ivy was down here with her and see how the future developed. This attraction with Ethan was happening so fast!

They rose together and Ethan wrapped his arms around her. Summer edged up onto her toes and they dissolved into their own world with a long and rewarding kiss of exploration.

'That's more like it,' he murmured. 'See you Saturday,' he called out as he walked away.

As always, a little of her heart went with him each time he left, but his comment jolted her into action. Saturday — the fête! The school visit today had delayed her preparations.

She needed to focus and not get distracted by a charismatic grazier. All the same she couldn't deny she was lapping up the experience.

* * *

Dozens of large white tents and green and white display gazebos covered the acres of Karingal Park lawns, some under trees, others in pools of sun. The record-breaking crowd, arriving in multitudes, blitzed the committee's expectations. Enticed to a social outing by Victoria's extravagant publicity and the magnificent weather still holding before the predicted storm, the locals opened their wallets to support the community and lingered from early morning until dusk.

Trade was brisk, including Summer's stall of fresh fruit, preserves, eggs, bunches of roses, perfumed bouquets of lavender and pungent bunches of herbs.

A percentage of all proceeds was donated to a fund for local projects.

Summer divided her time between her own stall and the CWA catering tent. Jean remained cooler since Summer's outspoken challenge at the committee meeting, but chatted easily enough when she appeared in the tent, and welcomed her help. Summer didn't regret not having bitten her tongue the day of the meeting at Karingal Park, but hoped they could still be friends. Their eating area under canvas bustled with volunteers and most tables were continually full with customers.

In the work area, Julie Williams and Summer worked side by side.

'I've never whipped so much cream and served so many Devonshire teas or soup and sandwiches in my life before.'

Earlier in the day, Julie had commented, 'You must be hectic working between two tents. Want me to mind your stall if you need a break?'

'Yes, that would give me a chance for a wander around. But what about your children?'

'Oh . . . ' Julie waved a hand, 'Lonnie

minds them while I'm in here but they're only interested in food and the giant bouncy castle, or riding the mini train. It's a big hit with the ankle biters.' She laughed.

At a distance Victoria strutted about, puffed with importance, surprisingly composed for the official opening mid-morning, slim and chic in a floating sapphire dress that she topped with a sweeping white mesh hat dipping across her forehead. The image of the society lady she wished to portray.

Ethan spent the morning showing off Brewster at the sheepdog demonstrations in a nearby paddock. He briefly appeared for the formal ceremony when he stood, handsome and genial, beside his mother. Meredith hovered in the wings, curiously never far from Summer's line of vision throughout the day. A coincidence, perhaps?

Because he was busy as host and in demand as a volunteer, Summer hardly saw Ethan all day except from a distance, but they exchanged frequent smiles and waves. She noticed he took turns manning the spinning wheel of fortune for the Rotary Club.

'I didn't realise he was a member,' she said to Julie later.

'Ethan's a staunch community member in most organisations. Landcare, Apex, Rotary, the sheep breeders and woolgrowers of course, and on the school council.'

Summer was surprised. 'But he doesn't have a family.'

Julie shrugged. 'Seems to love kids. Also means there are not too many nights he's forced to be at home with his mother.' She chuckled.

Summer thought her offhand remark disappointing. 'I know Victoria has a problem but I think it's sad, don't you?'

'Sure but often you can't help people unless they get so low they seek the help themselves.'

'Yes, you're right.' Summer sighed in frustration, for Ethan as much as his mother. 'Seems a contradiction, doesn't it?'

'Looks sober enough today, though,' Julie remarked.

'Maybe keeping busy helps.' Summer wondered if that was the answer and decided to mention it to Ethan sometime. Victoria shone in public. It was a shame to waste her energy and charm. There must be some constructive purpose she could be channelled toward.

The only minor annoyance of the day was an occasional willy-willy rushing through the garden, swirling up spirals of dust and leaves, causing squeals of anxiety as people clutched at their displays, forced to more securely anchor fluttering tablecloths and tent flaps.

After the excitement of one such short-lived windstorm, Summer was checking her produce had come to no harm in the upset and took advantage of a rare quiet moment to admire Ethan from afar.

'You're not the first.'

Summer spun around, recognising the sound of Meredith's smug tones. 'I'm sorry?' She frowned.

'There have been many other women in his life.'

Ah, so that's it — a crushed Meredith come to intimidate.

'I'd be stunned if there weren't.'

After a long and uncomfortable pause, at least on Summer's part because she suspected Meredith's appearance was not without purpose, the other woman straightened and with a superior air, said, 'He always comes back to me, you know.'

Summer was about to respond with a challenge but Meredith added, 'You see, we grew up together. We know everything about each other.'

Really? Someone should tell Ethan, for Summer doubted he was aware of the fact. She realised she was supposed to be discouraged at this, however, and wisely stayed silent, patiently anticipating the rest of the onslaught she was sure to come.

'It has happened fast for you, am I right?'

'He's certainly been most neighbourly

and helpful,' Summer admitted, playing along.

'He swept you off your feet. Spends every spare moment with you.'

'That's Ethan. Generous to a fault,' was all Summer could reply, starting to feel sick in the stomach at the direction of the conversation.

'I should warn you,' Meredith swept on with confidence in her presumed place in Ethan's life, clearly believing she had the upper hand. 'You can stop taking advantage of his unselfish nature. He never could ignore a needy single woman.'

To an extent, Meredith was right. Ethan had done so much for her in recent weeks, but what had she done for him in return? Was she guilty of exploiting his kindness? If so, it had been unintentional. He was simply always there and offering.

As poised as she could be in the daunting circumstances, Summer studied Meredith, whose glossy red mouth pulled into a creamy smile. 'Careful, lest you be labelled a gold digger.' Her silken voice lowered.

It was hard for Summer to hear. But so far Ethan didn't seem to have a problem with who she was and where she came from.

'Your envy is showing, Meredith,' Summer couldn't help herself replying.

Meredith's bony shoulder lifted in a careless non-committal gesture. 'We find that some women tend to get grand ideas about Ethan when they're not in his class,' she murmured, before slipping away as quietly as she had appeared.

The unpleasant encounter with Meredith left a normally sunny and positive Summer shaken. In the end, she concluded the spiteful woman's reasons stemmed from a misguided sense of reality. Perhaps, like Victoria, she was simply another unhappy rich woman? Bitter because Ethan had released her from the bond they once shared.

From all accounts, Meredith had a glamorous and successful life in

Sydney. How could she possibly be jealous of Summer? It set her wondering if the woman had frightened away all previous comers.

Still reeling from Meredith's venom, her attention was caught by the wonderful sight of Ethan striding her way, his sandy hair ruffled by the wind that had steadily strengthened during the afternoon.

'I noticed you were having a chat with Meredith.'

She managed a generous smile. 'Yes.'

He frowned. 'Everything all-right?'

Summer nodded, thinking quickly before responding, 'Just . . . getting better acquainted.'

She had certainly received a speedy lesson on the vindictive side of human nature. Thank goodness the woman lived far away and she wouldn't see her often.

'You look bushed,' he said softly, wrapping an arm about her shoulder and giving it a squeeze.

'It's been a long day.' From that

single gesture of comfort, he restored her calm and nothing else mattered. But Meredith's evil words still lurked in the back of her mind. In time, they would fade, but for now they remained raw, leaving her disturbed.

'At least the weather held off for the day,' Ethan remarked, his narrowed gaze fixed on the brooding grey sky, thick swells of cloud slowly moving in from the west. 'Our spring weather can be so unpredictable. Heatwave one week, hail stones the next and we'll be lighting up the fireplaces again.'

'It would be wonderful for the gardens if we get rain.' Summer glanced behind them at her depleted stall. 'I'd best get this lot sorted and head home to check the animals.'

The crowds had thinned and a slow procession of cars were leaving the property.

'Need any help?'

Remembering Meredith's words, Summer said brightly, 'No. Thanks for offering but this won't take long. Most of my produce was sold so there's not much left to pack. Besides, I'm sure you have heaps to do.'

'It's been a really successful fête this year.' He pushed a hand through his hair and stretched.

Summer nodded. 'It was well supported. All of Wombat Creek and half the surrounding district was here. It made all the work worthwhile.'

He bent down and pressed a light kiss on her mouth. 'See you soon,' he murmured and strode away.

But not before Summer noticed Meredith's icy glare in her direction. Too weary to care what the rejected woman thought, Summer packed her remaining produce into boxes and loaded Blossom.

Helping the CWA ladies fold up tables and chairs before she left, Jean Miller edged closer and said in an undertone, 'Ethan seems to have taken a liking to you.'

Had she seen them kiss? Summer wondered. She smiled and answered,

'He's a good friend and great company.'

'Must be all off with Meredith then?' Jean fished for gossip, giving the impression that Summer was moving in, pushing the other woman out.

Summer grinned to herself. This was going to test their friendship again. 'Why don't you ask him?' she suggested, all innocence.

Jean looked abashed. 'Oh, I couldn't do that.'

'At least, if you really need to know, he would tell you the truth,' Summer said and left it at that.

She had no intention of breaking Ethan's confidence and fuelling Jean's tendency to gossip. It seemed important for the woman to know everything and pass it on, but Summer had little tolerance for rumours and whispers. Didn't people have better things to do with their lives?

She knew it was normal and even accepted in a small community, so she held her tongue and made an excuse to leave.

12

Hurtling back toward Greenbanks in the van after the fête, its windows wound down to catch any breeze since the air had grown so humid before the coming storm, Summer longed to feel refreshed.

After she had checked her hens were safely roosted for the night, she wandered past the alpaca paddock. Serenity and Tinkerbell were safely sheltered with the other animals against the rising wind under the clump of trees at the bottom of a hill.

Warm blusters of air tugged at her long cotton skirt and she lifted the hair off her neck, pulling it over one shoulder. Idly spotting the dam, glinting and beckoning in the fading twilight, Summer wondered if she dared brave a swim. A slow smile spread across her face and she ambled closer.

The sticky air lay like a heavy shawl across her skin. She hadn't skinny-dipped in years. The idea of sliding into the water as naked as a newborn was too enticing to resist, so she cast off her clothes on the grass and waded into the dam. The wild sultry night was made for indulging the senses. Who would be out on such a night anyway?

★ ★ ★

Ethan scowled at the darkening sky alive with the first growling rolls of thunder. Unfriendly black clouds banked to the west and the evening was stifling. He climbed from his Ute in the garage at the side of the homestead. After driving around his recently shorn stud flocks, he was about to head indoors to see what he could rustle up for a meal in the kitchen but some instinct made him hesitate.

He remembered Amos lamenting the rusting sections of roof at Greenbanks and his inability with age and declining health to repair them. Ethan had been unable to investigate mending it before the old man died.

No longer fighting his constant thoughts of Summer, Ethan frowned at the mounting wind powering its way through the tops of the old immense mature trees in the garden. Anchored by a century of giant roots but far enough away from the homestead to avoid major damage if limbs broke and were flung to the ground.

He didn't share the same optimism for Summer's cottage, so he revved his vehicle into life again and headed west. Turning down the long lane toward Greenbanks, he shot a troubled glance through the windscreen, hoping he had enough time. Pushed by a building foul west gale, the change was approaching fast.

The tyres skidded in the gravel as he braked hard to a stop and leapt up onto the cottage veranda, rapping on the closed front door.

'Summer?' No response. He hunkered

down and patted Laddie, stretched out with his head on his paws, watchful. No doubt Misty was cowering somewhere inside. 'Where's she gone, boy?'

He strode around the house, checking the orchard beyond. Summer's van was parked nearby so she couldn't have gone far, but what on earth was she doing out of the house on a wild night like this?

He marched down toward the alpaca paddock away from the house. He halted, thinking he heard a sound. Listening again, he shook his head, stumped. It sounded like splashing. On a hunch, he headed downhill toward the dam.

When he caught sight of her, she was floating on her back, then rolled over and stroked out for a lap away from him. In the angry dusk, he watched the choppy currents of air make ripples on the surface of the dam. She hadn't seen his approach and remained oblivious to his presence. Incredibly, it looked as if she was swimming nude, because when her shoulders and back raised from the water, they were bare.

Scouting around, he glimpsed a pile of clothes on the grass. He shook his head and grinned, feeling guilty for staring but his male curiosity and attraction for this beautiful woman drew him to stay. At least he knew she was safe. He wasn't so sure about the house.

He sat, knees bent, arms crossed over them, feasting on her pleasure as she frolicked and splashed, letting his imagination fill in the blanks. Knowing Summer, her twilight swim would have been spontaneous.

It wasn't long before she stilled. The change was so sudden, he knew she was finally aware of his presence. Sinking up to her neck in the water, she slowly turned around.

'Ethan!' Her eyes doubled in astonishment and a playful grin spread across her mouth. 'Exciting night, huh?' She swam toward him. 'Why don't you join me?'

What an offer! But Ethan shook his head. 'I came to check your roof.'

She gave an amused and sensually throaty chuckle. 'A likely story.'

'Looks like this change will bring heavy rain. Leaking could be a problem at the cottage. Speaking of which . . . ' He held his arms out wide as the first fat drops made circles on the surface of the dam.

The rain only sprinkled them at first, smelling of musty dampness and promising more to come. Summer turned her face up to it, laughing, opening her mouth and letting the water drench her tongue. Then the heavens opened, engulfing them in a stinging torrent as the storm swept across the farm.

'This is madness,' Ethan yelled out across the water. 'Get out of the dam and back to the house.'

As Summer rose like a nymph from the dark shadowy water, Ethan turned away but not before catching a glimpse of her silhouette when a searing flash of lightning lit up the night.

After a moment, Summer said, 'You can look now. I'm decent.'

He looked back to see her eyes sparkling with fun, her wet hair plastered against her head and shoulders, her saturated clothes clinging to her body.

'That, Summer Dalton, I'm not sure you will ever manage to be.'

Her lofty expression suggested she might be stung by his words and he wondered if he should have phrased them differently.

'I didn't think I would be offending anyone by swimming on my own property,' she pointed out, licking rain from her lips.

'Who said you were offending anyone?'

'You disapprove.'

'Did I say so?'

'You're staring at me.'

'Ever considered that it might be in appreciation?'

'Is that what you call it?' She sounded sceptical. 'So, you're partial to a little spice, then?' she probed, teasing.

'I'm only human.'

'Such a relief,' she quipped.

Ethan admired Summer for having the courage to be her own person, swept with a flash of envy that he wasn't always entirely true to himself.

How could anyone imprison such a free spirit? Summer Dalton was an uninhibited woman, born to be thoroughly loved. A rush of protection overwhelmed him for the lively woman walking on ahead, saturated and bedraggled in the driving rain but jaunty with spirit in every step she took on the slick wet grass.

★　★　★

Summer's thoughts were far from positive as she trudged uphill, warm rain drenching every inch of her skin and clothes. Trust her to get caught. She had seen the scowl of disapproval on Ethan's face and feared because of her impulsive action, she may have lost his respect.

She almost regretted her impulse but

247

these bursts of spontaneity were in her nature, even if they might not be acceptable in Ethan's world.

To cover her regret, Summer swung around to face him, walking backwards uphill. 'You think I'm shameless, don't you?'

They stared at each other and something powerful other than the storm overhead stirred the loaded night air, crackling and fizzing with thunder and lightning.

'You're quite a temptress. And why are you mad at me?'

'I'm embarrassed you found me,' she admitted. 'And annoyed that you're being judgmental.'

'I haven't said a word.'

'You don't look pleased.'

'I'm thinking.'

'About my scandalous behaviour?'

'We always seem to end up in disagreement about something.' Ethan shook his head. 'How do you suppose we resolve that?'

Summer turned mischievous. 'We

could always make amends.'

She didn't know what induced her to do it but she halted while he caught up, standing directly in his path. He made no attempt to step aside. He, too, was drenched, fat beads of water clinging to his dripping hair, and his shirt clung to his chest like a second skin.

When he gently slammed into her, she gripped his wet clothes, gently rose on her toes and kissed him, no longer wanting to hide behind caution or propriety.

When she broke away, she said, 'I don't normally take liberties but I was raised to be honest about my feelings.'

'Which are?'

She shrugged. 'You're an attractive man.' As the rain teemed down even heavier, she dashed for the cottage again and shouted over her shoulder, 'What's not to like?'

Reaching it together, they leaped onto the porch, water streaming from their bodies into lakes at their feet. Laddie stood up and barked at their sudden appearance.

'Wait here.'

Summer retrieved thick towels from the adjoining laundry. Ethan had removed his shirt and was leaning out over the garden, wringing it out. The evening was turning cool and Summer shivered. Wrapping one huge towel around herself, she thrust the other at Ethan. He disappeared underneath it as he towelled his hair.

Once inside the cottage, the drumming rain sounded as noisy as stones being thrown onto the tin roof. Thunder cracked overhead and lightning flashed in through the window. Summer tried the light switches but nothing happened.

'Power's out,' she sighed.

In the gloom, she edged her way into the kitchen for a taper from the utility drawer then moved through the house lighting all of her candles on windowsills, tables and mantels until the cottage flickered with their soft glow, revealing Misty licking herself on a living room chair.

Ethan stood across the room, trousers in one hand, the towel wrapped around his waist. 'I'll light a fire and get these dry,' he offered. 'You should change before you catch a chill.'

She nodded, shaking with cold and retreated to her room. Meanwhile, Ethan prowled the house inspecting for leakage. He found buckets and dishes, placing them about the cottage to catch the drips. Enough to be annoying but, all the same, to be safe in case the weight of the water collapsed the ceiling, he didn't think it wise for her to stay here.

She reappeared in baggy cotton trousers and a soft loose jumper to find a roaring warming fire blazing and steam drifting from Ethan's clothes draped over chairs in front of it.

Half-dressed, he dashed out to his four-wheel drive and grabbed his oilskin Drizabone. When he didn't immediately return, Summer frowned until she heard thumping on the roof.

Ethan was up there in this weather?

And he'd been worried about a romp in the dam? She fumed and held her breath. That iron roof would be as slippery as glass.

When he returned, she flung at him, 'What were you thinking, climbing up there in this storm?'

He kissed her into silence against any further protest. 'Can't do any more tonight. I've put my small tarpaulin over part of it against the worst of the weather but you're coming back to the homestead with me overnight until this storm passes and the SES can repair the roof.'

'Is that necessary?'

'No argument.' He stalled any protest. 'I'm not taking any chances. I'll bring you back in the morning.'

'Your mother will have something to say about that.'

Ethan hedged. 'She's gone to a Melbourne concert.'

They would be alone together in that great house?

When she hesitated, Ethan barked,

'Go pack a bag. Scoot!'

'Your clothes aren't dry yet.'

'I'll put them on damp.'

'Bossy,' Summer muttered, but she obeyed, hiding a secret smile at his warmth and caring.

★ ★ ★

Although the worst of the storm had moderated by the time they reached Karingal Park, rain had drenched the land, creating torrents of rushing water in the gravelled roadside gutters. It glistened on grass and plants and the leaves of sagging branches in Ethan's vehicle headlights as they drew up before the house, looming dark and brooding in the starless night.

Brewster sat expectantly on the front veranda. Recalling Victoria's ban on the dog in the house, Summer gaped when Ethan coolly let his loyal animal trot indoors after him. By the way he waited patiently by the door, it appeared he expected to be admitted. Secret men's business while Victoria was away?

Catching her glance of wry amazement, Ethan quipped darkly, 'It's my home, not a five star hotel.'

'I didn't say a word,' Summer murmured as they all trundled into the dry warmth of the spacious entry hall.

'I'll show you up to a guest bedroom first, so you can dry off and change, then we'll raid the kitchen for something to eat,' he said over his shoulder, scooping up her small overnight bag and heading upstairs.

Summer followed, gaping at the portraits lining the walls and landing, and the deep red carpet muffling their footsteps to the upper floor.

Her room was as big as the whole of Greenbanks cottage and boasted its own huge bathroom with fluffy towels and a soft double bed — she knew because she bounced on it, grinning.

She sighed over the romantic window seat scattered with chintz cushions. Talk about a dream room! She had never known such indulgent comfort, and it was so cosy and safe on such an appalling night. Briefly, having never being exposed to such material wealth, she felt awed and unworthy.

'I'll be down in the kitchen getting dinner started,' Ethan told her indulgently. 'Come down when you're ready. Just turn right at the bottom of the stairs.'

When Ethan left, Summer moved across to the window. The storm still raged outside and fearsome winds hurled the huge old trees about in the garden. Drifts of pelting rain lashed against the window panes, rivulets running down in spidery paths. Streaks of lightning flashed across the wild night sky. In daylight and better weather, Summer imagined the view across the countryside from up here would be magnificent.

Lazily entranced by such luxury, she curled up on the window seat and watched the battering storm, contemplating Ethan and his sturdy bluestone house, both so strong and dependable.

No one had ever made her feel so safe and protected before. For a change, someone else was looking out for her and it felt good.

When Summer finally sauntered down to the kitchen, it was to find Ethan standing over a huge pot of boiling water and wielding a nasty knife, dicing chicken and vegetables. This tough male was domesticated, too, and looked so sexy with a towel slung over his shoulder, his thick hair darkly damp and still ruffled.

'I'm impressed. What are we eating?' Summer said to cover the awkward first moment of her appearance in a strange environment.

'Chicken kebabs and rice with a packet of salad.'

'Too easy.'

Ethan grinned. 'That's why I make it. I'm used to looking after myself when Victoria's away. I haven't starved yet.'

With his directions, she found cutlery and crockery to set the table in the bay window dining area, then she helped him slice chunks of fresh fruit for later. He turned on the barbeque plate built into the kitchen bench, glazed the meat and vegetable pieces and began to grill.

They worked in harmony organising the meal, but a taut thread of tension strained between them. Long silences mixed with snatches of conversation. They both seemed relieved when the meal was ready and they could concentrate on eating.

They were half finished before Ethan eventually asked, 'When do you plan on bringing Ivy down?'

'As soon as I get the roof fixed and I can arrange for someone to check on the animals for a few days while I'm away. With packing up and saying goodbyes to family and friends, I'll be away a week or more.'

'If I can help in any way, let me know.'

'Actually,' she hesitated, not wanting to offend him. 'I considered asking Sam. He lives close by and it will keep him occupied, make him feel needed. He must get lonely.'

Ethan nodded. 'Makes sense. I look forward to meeting your daughter when she's settled.'

When Summer glanced up to see his gaze of hope, the inference was clear. He wanted to be a part of both their lives. But with an antagonistic mother and bitter ex-girlfriend hovering in the wings, Summer predicted difficulties ahead. She just wanted peace in her life — especially for Ivy. At times, she still couldn't push past her own private doubts of any relationship succeeding with Ethan.

He set down his knife and reached out to cover her hand with his own, correctly reading her reservations. 'One day at a time, okay?'

'Thanks,' she whispered. 'I'm going to need it.'

Normally optimistic, she desperately wanted to trust and believe in this man and what he offered, and not anticipate trouble — but, first and foremost, it was her duty and obligation as a mother to protect her child and not expose her to undue friction.

She knew life wasn't all sugar sweet and at some point she had to trust her instincts again. She would cope. She smiled her reassurance at Ethan, letting her gaze sweep over this desirable and supportive man.

Knowing him better, she'd let down her guard a little and he had slowly revealed more about himself, too. Reassuring. Ethan wasn't Billy, and the generous grazier had proved he was nothing less than honourable.

'I can hear the cogs turning in your mind.' Ethan tried for humour but sounded anxious instead.

'It's a lot to take in. I see all this — ' she glanced around the gleaming timber and white kitchen — 'and wonder what you possibly see in me, in us. Our worlds are as far apart as could possibly be. But,' she dipped her glance, braving the words, needing him to know, 'I'm deeply attracted to you and, as you said, we should take it one step at a time.'

He wiped his brow of mock sweat. 'Phew. That's a relief. And I really do understand that you are still living under the cloud of your past,' he admitted reluctantly.

'Letting go is often the scariest part.'

'I'm surprised to hear that from you. You're the only person I know who embraces life and gives love so freely.' He stroked his thumb over the back of her hand in a soft caress. 'I never knew that joy until I met you. I'm glad to say, some of it has rubbed off on me.'

With the future looking rosy, they rinsed their dishes in the sink and took bowls of fruit and ice cream to the deep sofas in the lounge. Heavy drapes across the French windows kept the chill blustery night at bay, the indoors snug and warm. Brewster settled on a rug by the lit open fire, yawning and bored, but raised his head from his paws occasionally, ears pricked, to check up on his companions.

'What's your next step at Greenbanks?' Ethan asked later as he sipped coffee and Summer drank a huge mug of herbal tea.

'Find a market for that gorgeous fleece from my girls. I'm so tempted to spin it then have it knitted up into luxury garments.' She shrugged. 'But selling it raw will be quicker and help with my cash flow. Until I'm better established and my alpaca herd increases, I need to be cautious.'

'You'll do fine. You have a natural love and instinct for the land.'

Warmed by his compliment and the hot drink, they nestled closer together, the angry storm still pounding mercilessly outside. Now and again, the fire crackled and a glowing ember resettled itself in the grate.

The next thing she knew, Ethan's whispered voice was tickling her ear. 'You keep falling asleep on me. Am I so boring?'

Her eyes fluttered open and she stretched. His long kiss stirred her awake and her arms slithered up around his neck.

'Never.' She pressed another deep kiss to his mouth.

If only he knew! Knowing she was so

deeply cared for allowed her to relax. Summer found it liberating for someone else to take charge.

Ethan responded with deeper passion and they enjoyed each other a while longer until he sighed and drew away.

'You're exhausted, that's the problem. Sure you're not pushing yourself too hard on the farm?'

'There's been a lot to get sorted,' she protested.

He stood and easily scooped her up into his arms.

'I love it when you spoil me, Mr Bourke.' She nuzzled his neck.

He kissed her on the nose and began climbing the stairs. 'You're welcome, Ms Dalton.'

13

Summer woke, momentarily disoriented until she remembered last night. Ethan carrying her to this room, a few more luscious and lingering kisses before he deserted her. The luxury of a deep, hot bath and a thick, white robe.

Feeling pampered, she resisted the temptation to disappear beneath the doona again, forget the world and her responsibilities and go back to sleep. Instead she eased back the warm cover, sat up and pushed her heavy hair back over her shoulders.

She crossed to the windows and drew aside the drapes. Weak sunlight washed over the damp, glistening garden. The rain had stopped. Finally. Hearing a car door slam and voices, she leaned forward and knelt on the window seat, peering down to the driveway below.

Summer pulled back with a gasp,

startled. Victoria was home!

Against her will, it bothered her what Ethan's mother would think when she learned Summer had stayed overnight. No doubt the woman would assume the worst, and read more into her presence than the truth. She might even be prepared to believe Summer had engineered her stay while Victoria was away.

Summer wavered over whether to go down and help Ethan explain, but then realised he hardly needed her support. She had seen him handle his mother.

Nonetheless, Summer pulled on the fluffy robe, ran a brush through her hair and walked along the landing, not exactly sure what she planned to do. Hearing raised voices drifting up from below, she hesitated, suddenly feeling like an intruder and wracked with guilt for sitting on the top step and eaves-dropping.

★　★　★

'You're home a day early, Mother,' Ethan observed.

Victoria threw her plush woollen coat carelessly aside and headed for the well-stocked bar in the sitting room. As she tossed in ice cubes and splashed in drink, she snapped, 'I tried calling last night to let you know but the lines were down.'

'I know. They're still out. I'm sure they'll be reconnected this morning.' Watching his mother's fidgety pacing, he asked, 'Something wrong?'

She swilled her drink and hesitated, turning her back on him to look out on the bleak rain-washed garden. 'We went to a lovely new little restaurant at Docklands,' she said with contempt. 'But the food was simply unacceptable. You know I can't abide incompetence . . . ' She trailed off vaguely, waving a limp arm in the air.

Ethan silently groaned. He was willing to bet that Victoria had caused trouble. 'And?'

His mother swung around, glaring.

'When I complained, they had the audacity to suggest I leave. And, worse — ' she exploded with venom. 'Barbara and Tom had the nerve to agree! They went off and left me, stranded. My best friends!' she almost shrieked. 'Then they phoned me this morning at the apartment and cancelled all our plans. The gallery, shopping, everything. I mean, what was the point of staying?' she raged, gulping the rest of her drink and pouring herself a refill.

Ethan sank his hands into his trouser pockets and suggested gently, 'It's still early. Do you really think you should have another drink?'

She whirled on him. 'I'm your mother, not your child.' Her narrowed gaze swept the room like a hawk seeking prey. 'You've had a visitor!'

For a moment, he thought she meant Summer and was primed to explain until she added, 'There are paw prints all over the floor. You've had that wretched dog in here. How could you?'

she spluttered. 'When you know I forbid it.' She raised her voice, growing volatile. 'Look at all the dirt in the house.'

Exasperated and losing patience, Ethan said sharply, 'I don't know why you're upset, Mother. It's not as if you have to clean it yourself. If it bothers you, I'll mop the tiles as soon as I get a chance. And lower your voice. We have a guest.'

'Who?'

'Summer Dalton.'

'What on earth is that unsatisfactory girl doing under my roof?' Victoria flew into an uncontrolled rage.

'She's my guest. And she's taking refuge from the storm.' He calmly explained about the storm and damage to the cottage roof but clearly his mother didn't believe him, or even care.

'You couldn't have chosen a more disreputable person to stay under my roof,' she roared.

'On the contrary, Mother.'

'Everyone will talk.' She gasped in horror. 'The gossip!'

'For goodness' sake, Mother, no one knows except you and I.' He dismissed her flimsy exaggeration.

'You'd better hope not.' She glared at him with narrowed eyes. After a telling pause, she accused, 'I suppose you slept with her.'

'That's none of your business and an invasion of my privacy. My friendship with Summer has nothing to do with you, but just for the record, no, Mother, I didn't.'

'You're lying,' she scoffed, and rushed on. 'I can't believe you'd put yourself in a such compromising situation — and with David Dalton's daughter, of all people.'

'How David and Eleanor choose to live their life is their choice. Personally, I don't see anything wrong with peace, love and freedom, do you?' His low voice and fixed gaze met her challenge.

'You've been brainwashed by that loose woman.' Victoria flung an arm high. 'What were you thinking? I warn you, Ethan, keep away from her. She's not for you. She'll ruin our image.'

Ethan shook his head sadly and pushed out a sigh of frustration. 'You mean *your* image, Mother.'

'You're heir to a prosperous pastoral station. You have a position to uphold in your family and in the community. People look up to us and respect us. They expect certain standards,' she gushed importantly. 'If you must be indiscreet, at least keep it secret.'

Ethan studied the sad, vindictive woman his mother had become and couldn't believe her veiled suggestion. 'You don't get it, do you, Mother?' He said quietly. 'You never have.'

'Get what?' she yelled.

'People,' Ethan said and half-turned, disgusted, ready to stride away.

'No. *You* don't get it,' she threatened and stepped closer, her hard eyes glittering. 'I can take all this away from you, just like that.' She snapped her fingers in his face.

Ethan stilled in disbelief. 'What exactly are you saying?'

'This property is still in my name. I can withhold your inheritance. You'll get nothing.'

'Why? Because of Summer?'

'Give up that woman or give up Karingal Park!' She flung down her ultimatum like a challenge.

In a heartbeat, Ethan could see ten years of hard labour snatched away from him, stunned at the depths of his mother's cruel intent. Thrown by her threat but undaunted, he knew he could call her bluff and did a swift mental calculation.

He had his own stud rams and flock of breeding ewes. He could walk away, no regrets, and leave this woman who had given him life to slowly sink into an oblivion of her own making.

Or he could stay and take a stand; see she received the help she so desperately needed. With flying threats like the one she had just given, she was growing more neurotic every day. But he knew it was only her drunken stupor talking.

He would need to tread cautiously.

Humour her, but insist on rehabilitation, however long it took. It would need discussion with Summer, but he knew she would understand.

But first he needed to calm his mother down.

'All right, Mother. You win.'

He didn't add, *for now*, but in his own mind that was implicit.

Time enough later to reveal the truth and the strength of his feelings for Summer and his hope for a future with her. Victoria wouldn't be able to deal with that fact at the moment, not while she was so hysterical.

He would explain after she had agreed to some form of treatment or therapy, when the chances of her being more receptive were greater. He wasn't sparing her feelings, just waiting to get his timing right.

Summer had opened the doorway to the future for him, making him realise it could be with no one else but her.

Victoria gaped at him in astonishment. 'You'll give her up?'

'If that's what you want.' He cringed as he lied. 'Yes.'

★ ★ ★

Summer had heard enough. Shocked at Ethan's betrayal and with a hand over her mouth to stifle her incredulous gasps, she quietly backed up the stairs and swiftly packed her small bag. Trying to stem her tears, she hastily left by the back staircase and side door.

Last night had seemed so real and genuine. She wouldn't have thought Ethan capable of such deceit and disloyalty. She could have sworn his hormones were raging as fast as hers last night. Apparently it had only been lust on his part, and not genuine affection after all.

She now ached for a man she could never have. Would she have fitted into his fancy world and conservative ways, anyhow? Trying to lessen her misery, she told herself it could never have worked.

To save time and avoid being seen, she bypassed the gravelled driveway and headed across the homestead paddock to join the main road further down. At the property fence, she tossed over her bag then squeezed between the wires and continued her trek toward home.

With every angry stride of disappointment, Summer retraced every moment she had spent with Ethan last night. Nothing. She could think of nothing in his behaviour that gave any impression he had been using her. But he must have been, otherwise why would he have buckled so easily to his mother's pressure?

She could still hear Ethan's words, *You win*.

Summer had been convinced he was made of stronger stuff. Apparently money talked far more loudly in a blueblood's world. When it came to the crunch, she was no competition for the holy dollar. It cut her deeply to think she had fallen for being used — again.

She smacked her forehead in frustration and self-recrimmination.

'How could I have been so gullible?' she railed into the cool morning air.

★ ★ ★

Ethan bounded upstairs. 'Summer?'

He tapped lightly on the guest room door, slightly ajar. When there was no response, he pushed it open. The bed was crumpled but empty and Summer's overnight bag gone. Scratching his sandy hair, he wondered if she had left in deference to his mother's arrival.

With no vehicle, unless she hitched a lift with a passing local, she would be walking. Feeling annoyed at her stubborn independence but understanding her possible reason, he also marvelled at her spirit. He would find her, then return to finish his conversation with his mother.

Downstairs in the hall, he ran into Sally arriving for her weekly housekeeping. 'Morning, Ethan.'

274

'Ah, Sally.' He jingled his car keys absently in his pocket. Perfect timing. The dilemma of trying to be in two places at once was solved. 'Just the person I need. Could you head over toward Greenbanks and pick up Summer? She'll probably be about a kilometre down the road by now.' Sally frowned and opened her mouth but Ethan just shook his head and said, 'Don't ask. And then could you stay and help her tidy up after the storm? Her cottage suffered damage last night. The SES will be out to fix her roof but she might appreciate a hand indoors.'

'Now?'

He nodded, adding, 'Don't worry about your work here today, Sally. It can wait until later.'

'But Mrs Bourke — '

'You let me deal with her.'

Sally stepped back, eyes wide. 'All right, sir. I'll see you next week.'

On his way back to the kitchen, Ethan's thoughts were on Summer. He winced in shame that she felt obliged to leave, and would once more need to apologise for his mother.

Not for much longer, he vowed, scowling. Matters had reached a crisis point and Victoria's days of permanent residence at Karingal Park were numbered, he feared. At the least, they would be limited.

Despite the morning's chaos, his mind drifted to nicer memories and he managed a smile. He had enjoyed thoroughly kissing Summer last night until they had both wanted more. Despite her reservations, for which he was prepared to give her any amount of time she needed, she was a woman made for the country and family life.

Once he'd sorted out his mother, he fully intended taking full advantage of Summer's buried feelings and give them a little nudge by heading over to Greenbanks and reassuring her how he felt, convince her their strong attraction would work.

If he was being honest, he'd been sold on his gorgeous and caring new neighbour ever since that first moment they met on the slope in front of the house the day she arrived.

His smile vanished when he confronted his mother again in the kitchen. His only small consolation came from seeing her making coffee and not pouring another drink. Good. For what he had to say, he needed her lucid and sober.

She tossed him a smug conspiratorial smile. 'Has she gone?' At his curt nod, she added, 'Good riddance. We don't need her type here.'

Ethan knew it was the alcohol talking but her vicious insult still stung. 'You hardly know her, Mother. That's very uncharitable of you.'

She scoffed. 'The Dalton's girl's reputation was ruined long ago.' She brushed aside his disagreement. 'What's one more slur on her character? Not that she had any reputation to start with, I'm sure. It's only a matter of time before a disreputable girl like her would leave anyway — Really, Ethan, you need to stop dallying with all the local riff-raff and find a worthy wife. What about Meredith? You can make it up with her.'

'Meredith is your choice, Mother, not mine.'

'Make amends with her,' she pleaded.

'No.'

She glared at her son in horror. 'I've always thought — '

'I know what you thought, Mother. That you could manipulate me like you did with Father but where has it got you? Your selfish demands have only ruined your life and made it difficult for everyone around you. You don't seem to care who you hurt in the process.'

Ethan's voice lowered to soft appeal. 'Despite all your efforts to control everyone around you, it didn't bring you happiness, did it? You're miserable and you won't even admit it.'

He stepped forward and gently gripped her shoulders. 'Mother, you're not well. You need help, someone to talk to. I think it would be better for everyone if you live in your city apartment while you sort yourself out.'

Victoria gave a bitter laugh. 'You mean see a shrink.'

Ethan shrugged. 'Seems to me you have little left to lose.'

'I've tried before, remember?' She slumped onto a kitchen stool and glanced up at him, weary, her spirit broken. This was the first time his mother had been even remotely approachable in a long time.

'Then we'll try harder. Together,' he said gently.

'I've just had a rough weekend,' she groaned defensively. 'I'll have a rest and then I'll be fine, you'll see.'

'No, Mother. Not this time.'

'You just want to turn me out.' Her veined eyes pooled with tears. Victoria Bourke was never this vulnerable, nor had he seen her so low.

'Of course not. This will always be your home. But you need to sort yourself out, Mother. You'll never listen to anyone in the family, so perhaps an outsider is your best chance?'

'For what?' she said miserably. 'Why?'

'So you can live life with dignity. I should think you'd want that for yourself — you of all people.'

While she gaped at him as though his words had finally registered, Ethan said, 'When you've had your coffee go and take a shower. When I get back, we'll make some decisions and set arrangements in motion.'

Victoria staggered to her feet as her son left the room. 'Where are you going?' she shouted after him.

'Out.' Ethan slammed the door behind him, needing some fresh air, frustrated with the person his mother had allowed herself to become.

He didn't hear his mother's whining voice. 'What about the floor?'

14

Summer heard a vehicle approaching and moved further over to walk on the grass, but didn't recognise Sally Miller until she pulled up alongside and wound down her window.

'Ethan said I'd find you along the way.'

'He did?'

'Yes. He said to tell you he'd call in later.'

Ethan Bourke was the last person she wanted to see. 'Why?'

'I didn't ask.' Sally was clearly taken aback by Summer's bluntness. 'I'm just heading over to your place. The boss said you needed some help this morning with cleaning up.'

'Oh, he did, did he?'

Confused and angry, Summer wondered why Ethan would dump her, then send someone over to help. *Always the generous benefactor*, she thought bitterly. Mr-Smooth-and-Charming — when it pleased him, that is, and making sure that everyone saw his good deeds in the community, helping the new arrival in the district.

'Hop in,' Sally urged, leaning across to open the passenger door.

Too upset to argue, Summer climbed in.

'Why didn't you wait for Ethan to drive you?'

'His mother returned home.' Summer crossed her arms, filled with gloom. 'Three's a crowd.'

'Yes, I saw her car.' Sally's face lit up. 'I say, did you and Ethan — '

'No!' Summer snapped, scowling. 'Absolutely not!'

Sally shrugged, grinning at the road ahead as they drove. 'If you say so. Mrs B will be furious I didn't come in today, so I hope Ethan sorts her out and explains. She likes everything immaculate, you see. I can't tell you the number of times I've had to do things a second time just because she's not satisfied.'

'Why do you work for her if she's so difficult?' Summer glanced away out the window as they neared home, dark on anything that involved the Bourkes at the moment.

'She pays top money,' Sally announced. 'And I'm saving like mad just now,' she added, clearly expecting her passenger to show interest and follow up on her teaser.

Half heartedly, Summer obliged with, 'Oh? For anything special?'

'My future,' she said excitedly.

Oh, the innocence of youth. Summer sighed, feeling old and jaded and wincing at the girl's bliss in the face of her own unhappiness. 'Sounds like you already have someone in mind.'

Sally groaned with pleasure. 'I sure do. Lordy, one pash with Corey Sanderson down the shearing shed and I knew he was the one for me. He's such a hunk,' she enthused. 'You should see his muscles in a black singlet when he's shearing. Enough to make a girl faint,' she sighed, fanning herself with one hand. 'He's away working at the moment. We both have two jobs, you see, saving like mad for a deposit for a place of our own.'

To Summer's relief and none too soon, Sally finally reached the gate and turned off the main road and onto the lane down to the cottage. It meant rescue from having to appear happy about someone else's euphoric romance when her own had just been completely shattered.

The State Emergency Service guys were already on the roof, properly securing the tarpaulin and clearing up minor debris that had been blown around the cottage during the storm.

The foreman, who introduced himself as Greg, descended a ladder to greet her. 'The roofers can come out tomorrow,' he told her. 'Not much needs replacing, so it shouldn't be a big job.'

She hoped not; she had no idea how

she would pay for it. Still dazed from the revelations at Karingal Park, Summer stood transfixed by the volunteer activity and the generosity and co-operation of everyone in reacting so quickly to her dilemma. Since Ethan was the only one who knew, he must have alerted them.

As Summer stammered out her thanks, the foreman said, 'All the services have been reconnected. Oh, and by the way, your phone's been ringing. Someone's been trying to call you while we were up on the roof.' He scrambled back up the ladder with a wave and a smile.

Sally followed Summer indoors. 'Wow, you've made this really nice.'

After a brief, curious inspection of the house and without any lingering, Sally immediately started emptying the containers filled with water from the leaking roof. Summer shook her head in amusement — Sally was a busy beaver like her mother.

She moved into the office and pressed the digits for missed calls. She recognised her parents' number and wondered why Eleanor or David had tried to get in touch. Summer's first anxious thoughts were for Ivy, and she she called New South Wales straight away.

She was alarmed to learn from Eleanor's explanation that Ivy's derelict father, Billy, had suddenly reappeared on the scene, wildly professing his right to custody of his abandoned daughter, claiming Summer had deliberately renounced all responsibility by moving to Victoria.

Summer gasped with fury. 'What a load of codswallop. She was in your care temporarily. How dare he question my fitness as a mother! I've been with her every day of her life except for the past few weeks. Did you explain why?' she demanded of her mother.

'You know Billy,' Eleanor said lamely. 'He never did listen.'

'That's no excuse,' Summer scoffed, pacing in the study. 'What about him? He disappeared the day I told him I was pregnant!'

'I know but now he's called the police and social services and it's getting messy with others involved.'

'Oh, for goodness' sake!' Summer was livid. 'He's created a dispute out of nothing.' Flooded with anger and distress, she clenched her fist, knowing she must immediately go back up north and rescue her daughter. 'Is Ivy with you now?'

'Yes.'

'Don't let her out of your sight. Where's Billy?'

'Hovering. Talking to the police.'

From the corner of her eye through the half open doorway, Summer noticed Ethan and Sally together talking. When had he arrived? Distracted, she tried to refocus on her telephone conversation.

'Okay, that's it. I'm done. I'm flying up today to get my daughter and make sure she's safe. I'll be there by nightfall. Don't you dare release Ivy to anyone, do you understand, Eleanor?'

'I'll do my best,' her mother said meekly, 'But there are threats flying in

287

all directions here.'

Terrified of losing Ivy to some misguided civil servant — or, worse, to Billy — Summer insisted on speaking to one of the police officers at her parent's place. She explained the situation in Victoria and that she would be there as soon as possible, reassured by the policewoman they would take no action until she arrived and that Ivy would not be removed from her grandparents' care.

Summer asked to speak to Ivy. When told her half sister, Skye, was amusing her in the house while the adults and authorities sorted the mess outside, Summer's mind eased. Poor little Ivy would be bewildered by all the chaos. She sighed. What were the odds of being dealt a double emotional dilemma on the same day?

Nervous and preoccupied, Summer finished on the telephone, then hurried into her bedroom to pack. Sally gingerly appeared in the doorway as Summer hastily stuffed clothes into a small bag and crammed a pile of important papers into a side pocket.

'Ethan's here. He wants a word.'

'I don't. I have nothing to say to him.'

Sally frowned, dithering. 'I doubt he'll take no for an answer.'

'Tough. Tell him to suck it up!' Summer pressed a hand to her forehead, closed her eyes and tried to focus. 'Sally, I need your help. I have a problem at home. I'm leaving in five minutes to fly back up north. Can you please call in on Sam Guthrie on your way home? Ask him if he could come over and supervise the roof tilers tomorrow and mind my animals for a few days?'

'Sure.' Sally nodded willingly.

Just then, Ethan barged into the room. 'Summer?'

Pulled in two directions, she did not acknowledge his presence and kept her head down, packing. 'I can't do this now, Ethan. I have to leave in a hurry. Sally will explain.'

Jolted by her bluntness, he sounded awkward. 'Can I help?'

Summer forced herself to meet his gaze. Hands on hips, gaping at her, he looked suitably bewildered but not in the least contrite. He had some nerve! How could he face her like this without hardly blinking an eye, as though nothing offensive and wounding had happened between them? Had he no shame?

'I can't deal with more than one catastrophe at a time. Right now, I need to leave here, quick sticks.'

Of all times, she needed his support now more than ever but she wouldn't ask for it. With an agonising hit of reality, she understood she might never have the opportunity or inclination again.

He frowned. 'You will be back, won't you?'

'Of course. I live here.'

No smooth talking blueblood would drive her out of her own home. Living nearby might make life sticky at times but she would survive.

At her statement, Ethan seemed less apprehensive, although why her life should be any concern of his now, she couldn't fathom. In her angst for Ivy, Summer didn't care. She zipped her bag, slung it over one shoulder and grabbed the van keys from the bedside table.

Scowling in thought, hoping she had remembered everything she needed to take, Summer brushed past Ethan, murmured a brief goodbye and thanks to Sally and left the farm.

Hurtling along the highway east to Ballarat, Summer sank into her own lonely thoughts, her only company on the four-hour journey. She pushed her noisy, struggling van to its limits on the freeway to Melbourne and the airport, chewing over her forced necessity to dip into her precious dwindling savings.

But this crisis was a real emergency and involved Ivy. All of her emotions were consumed and focused solely on her child. Ivy's well-being and the importance of bringing her back here to live had never been more important.

It didn't help to lecture herself for not doing it sooner. She was flooded with guilt at leaving her there at all, but who knew Billy would ever be such a wild card? Who could possibly have predicted such a radical turn of events? In all the upheaval of recent hours, try as she might, she wasn't only thinking of Billy.

Another more important man also occupied her thoughts.

* * *

That evening, Ivy huddled safely into her mother's arms at David and Eleanor's house after a touching reunion. Once her daughter was settled happily, playing with Skye, and reassured that Mummy wasn't leaving without her this time, Summer confronted Billy.

Normally calm, she blasted him with a piece of her mind and set both the police and the representatives of the local authorities straight. She produced a copy of the title deeds to Greenbanks and her grandfather's will to prove her reason for a temporary absence in Victoria and leaving her child.

At times, although she remained outwardly controlled, inside she shook with the fear of what might have happened.

Fortunately, it was soon proven that Billy's ridiculous accusations were nothing more than unsubstantial threats and his false allegations were quickly dropped. His unkempt appearance and idle ravings soon revealed him as an unfit father to even have access to his child anyway.

Her heart was heavy with pity for him as Summer watched the police lead Ivy's disgraced father away.

15

Worried about Summer's coldness toward him and her uncharacteristic state of anxiety when she left the cottage, which he sensed was separate from the issues that had arisen with Ivy, Ethan travelled behind her at a discreet distance all the way to Melbourne.

At the airport, he lurked in the background like a private investigator, until he discovered her flight information and booked himself a seat on the same plane at the rear.

At Coolangatta, he too hired a vehicle and tailed her south across the border and inland from Byron Bay all the way to her home town.

Directed by people in the main street when he lost her, Ethan easily found the house. Among other cars and police vehicles, he parked further along and walked along the overgrown rainforest pathway, wet and steamy from a recent downpour of rain.

Not wanting to intrude, he watched from the edge of the garden, in view but unnoticed with everyone caught up in the unfolding drama. His heart wrenched when Summer strode onto the scene thrusting a handful of papers at the police. They stepped aside, conferring to read them.

At one point, she confronted Ivy's father like a fierce lioness protecting her cub. Ethan's heart beat with love, impressed with her poise and pride. Only once did she slightly raise her voice and appear to lose control; nor did she need to — everyone listened.

A wild-looking young man — probably Billy, Ethan guessed — at first resisted police attempts to remove him but after a short while, he was submissively led away.

The situation seemed under control, so Ethan stayed in the background waiting to be noticed, hesitant to approach. A middle aged couple, lean and brown, both with long, straggly greying hair and loose baggy clothes, lingered on the veranda, surrounded by a variety of children. Presumably David and Eleanor, Summer's parents.

With the confusion over, Summer stood off to one side looking bleak and alone. He longed to move forward, to take her in his arms and comfort her but held back, unsure of his welcome.

Back home, she'd seemed upset with him about something unrelated to the problem with Ivy's father. He had no idea of her plans or how long she meant to stay up here but before he left town, they needed to talk.

His heart swelled with tenderness when he saw Summer's face light up at the sight of a small dark-haired child emerging from the house. Ethan smiled — this had to be Ivy, for the little angel was a miniature of her mother. Summer scooped up her daughter and hugged her tight.

★   ★   ★

Summer's intuition, always a mystery but strong nevertheless, made her aware of another presence. She tore her attention away from her parents standing beside her on the veranda, glancing toward the thick rainforest at the edge of the garden.

A man, hands deep in his pockets, stood by the thick trunk and roped roots of an ancient fig.

She sucked in a sharp breath, shocked to see him here of all places. Why on earth had he followed her halfway across Australia?

Their gaze held. Ethan's eyebrows flickered upward in question and his mouth melted into a smile. His presence bewildered and disarmed her, but she couldn't ignore what he had said.

He'd come all this way. But why?

Summer was stunned, struggling with her pull of attraction for him, and baffled by his appearance and what it meant for them. She couldn't move. Last she heard, he didn't want her, and now he'd shown up here?

After Billy's scare, her emotions were still raw and she felt vulnerable.

Still holding her apprehensive, clinging daughter, some stronger impulse moved her feet and drew her toward him.

She eventually found her voice and said, 'This is a surprise.'

'I care.'

The two words were said with such simple heartfelt honesty, how could she not believe him? But she had to wonder what had changed since this morning. Nothing had changed for her. She was still cursed by the same need and longing for a man it made no sense for her to love.

They stood in silence, assessing each other for a moment until he said, 'Aren't you going to introduce me?'

Summer looked down at her daughter and smiled, brushing the shining black hair back from her face. 'This is my daughter, Ivy . . . Ivy, say hello to Mr Bourke.'

'Hello,' Ivy said shyly, snuggling into

her mother and eyeing the strange visitor with caution.

'Pleased to meet you Miss Dalton. If it's okay with you, I'm going to kiss your mother.'

Convinced this must all be a dream, Summer didn't resist when Ethan leaned forward and planted a warm kiss on her mouth. Why would she? In spite of everything, her heart was still his.

'Mummy, I don't got no room.' Ivy squirmed between them.

'Sorry, Pumpkin.' Reluctantly, Summer moved away from the man who was making her feel hot and confused.

'We need to talk,' Ethan said bluntly.

Sounded promising, if puzzling, after his words of dismissal to his mother earlier today. Uncertain, she said, 'I won't leave Ivy.'

'I wouldn't expect you to. Bring her along.'

Before they left, Ethan walked over to Summer's parents, who stood gaping at them from the veranda, and introduced himself.

'Richard Bourke's boy.' David shook his hand warmly. 'Your father and I were friends once. A long time ago.'

Minutes later, Summer and Ivy piled into Ethan's rented vehicle and, after a short drive east to the coast, stopped for a huge order of fish and chips before heading for the beach.

The tranquillity of a streaked orange sunset over Byron Bay generated a sense of peace in Summer. She glanced across at her striking male companion and Ivy playing safely and happily nearby.

Right now, she felt like she would never let her precious daughter out of her sight ever again.

Ethan looked relaxed and handsome in shorts and a T-shirt, his sandals forsaken, toes half buried in warm sand. When he glanced over at her, his face shadowed with concern. She waited for him to voice what was on his mind.

'Why did you leave Karingal Park so suddenly this morning and why were you so cross with me at the cottage?'

Still troubled by memories of the conversation she'd overhead on the staircase, Summer explained.

Ethan groaned and cursed. 'You should have waited another five minutes.' Then he fully clarified, word for word as far as he could recall, the complete conversation with his mother, including the vital missing pieces. He detailed the reasons for needing to deceive his mother.

Flooded with relief that Ethan hadn't dumped her after all, Summer gasped in embarrassment at what she had done, shaking her head as she stammered out her apologies before he had barely finished.

'I'm so sorry for being so hasty in leaping to a wrong conclusion about you. I should know you better — I usually place more faith in people,' she assured him.

'I wish you'd felt able to trust me,' Ethan said softly. 'You must know how I feel about you.'

She grinned. 'I'm beginning to guess.'

'I'm going to need a lot of kisses to heal my wounded pride . . . '

She nodded and smiled. 'Done.'

She leaned closer, he leaned closer and their lips drifted together in what she knew was the first of what was going to be many doses of therapy in his rehabilitation.

Their gaze turned toward Ivy, squealing in delight as a wave rushed into the moat she had dug around a sand castle.

'She's a beautiful child,' Ethan said. 'Of course, you are her mother.'

Summer smiled indulgently, accepting the compliment.

'I hope she's not the only child in my life.' Summer sighed. 'I want more children some day, and Ivy should have brothers and sisters.'

'I hope you'll let me be their father,' Ethan suggested softly.

Summer's heart pounded as Ethan squinted out to the horizon defining the turquoise sea and pastel twilight sky.

He'd certainly hinted at a serious relationship before — but this?

He turned and let a gaze of gentle adoration settle on her and implored her, 'I'm offering you the works. The ceremony, the piece of paper that ties us together for a lifetime. I love you, Summer, and I want to marry you. If you'll have me.'

Still reeling at the incredible turn of events since this morning, she was even more stunned by his proposal.

'Are you sure you don't just want me for my dowry?' she teased. 'I'm worth marrying, you know. I have my own property.'

Ethan grew serious and after covering her mouth with a deep but gentle kiss, said softly, 'Oh, I know exactly what you're worth, Summer Dalton. I'd say you're pretty much priceless, actually.'

She took a deep, steadying breath. 'Are you sure you've thought this through properly? You're not just getting me, remember?'

Her gaze travelled to the water's edge where Ivy was scooping out another channel in the sand. 'It's pretty much a package deal. Me, Ivy, a herd of alpacas, my chooks, Misty, Laddie . . . '

Ethan groaned with mock indulgence. 'A woman once told me that alpacas make great sheep guards. I have no problem with transferring them over to Karingal Park paddocks. If you're agreeable, that is. It would be easier to care for them.'

'What about Greenbanks?'

'It's yours to do with as you please,' he shrugged. 'But personally, I think it would make a fabulous retreat or bed and breakfast, and we should be the first guests — on our honeymoon.'

Summer smiled and nudged him. 'You've been giving this a lot of thought, haven't you? But I defintely want to keep it, either way — for Ivy.' She glanced skyward. 'Grandfather would be pleased.'

'Meanwhile you could lease out the whole property for your own income.

You'd have to choose your tenants carefully, of course.'

Ethan's suggestion gave Summer an idea and she snapped her fingers. 'I know the perfect couple! Sally's a meticulous housekeeper. She and Corey could live there for as long as they want — or until Ivy's old enough to decide what she wants to do with it.'

They both turned reflective and their thoughts wandered to the old man who had been the catalyst for their meeting.

After a few moments' silence, Ethan prompted, 'So, how about it?'

'You mean the marriage thing?' Summer asked, and he nodded a little anxiously. 'But what about your mother? She'll certainly strongly object to what you have in mind.'

'She'll have to adjust.' He reached for her hand and linked their fingers together. 'Besides, I have plans for her that don't involve living in the homestead. Quite frankly, when she's better and more like herself, I doubt she'll want to anyway. The city apartment will be too hard to resist.'

'I don't know what to say.'

'Most people choose either yes or no . . .'

'It's a bit sudden . . . '

Ethan's eyes locked on hers and she could sense him holding his breath, wating for her answer. Suddenly her face broke into a smile as she said, 'Yes!'

Ethan let out a long sigh of relief and they collapsed onto the sand, laughing with happiness and kissing, intertwined with each other.

When they had recovered and Ivy had toddled up the beach to join them, Summer said wistfully, 'It's a daunting thought that we'll be living in that great big house of yours.'

'Our big house,' he corrected. 'We'll fill it up with playmates for Ivy and it won't seem so big. It'll be a family home . . . our family.'

Summer snuggled closer and wrapped her arms around his neck. 'What a grand idea.' After they kissed again, she frowned.

'So you won't mind if it gets a bit . . . well, untidy sometimes?'

'Lived-in is good.' Ethan laughed.

Ivy tugged at Ethan's shorts. 'Why are you kissing my mummy?'

'Because I love her.' He scooped her onto his knee.

'Why?'

'Because she's beautiful and special, just like you.'

'We're going to live in Gwampa's house,' she told him importantly. 'It's got woses in the garden. We don't got woses here, do we, Mummy?'

Summer and Ethan looked over the top of her small dark head and smiled at each other. Time enough to tell her about their slight change of plans later, when everything was settled.

Later, Summer watched Ethan gently support Ivy on her tummy, helping her to float as she kicked in the water. Then he held her hand as they waded back through the small waves and shallows toward her.

A rush of love and warmth for the

two of them was followed by a stirring of longing for this vibrantly alive man with whom she had deeply fallen in love and who was making her dream come true.

They were going to be a proper family. Since childhood, that was all she had ever wanted.

★ ★ ★

Four months later, Victoria Bourke briefly returned to Karingal Park as a guest for her son's wedding. Her absence on an extended holiday hadn't fooled any of the locals and, although it was never voiced, the residents of Wombat Creek had guessed the truth.

When Victoria had started tossing out directives that the wedding must be a grand affair and the couple married in the two-hundred-year-old bluestone church because Bourkes had always married there, Summer calmly announced, 'Well, I'm not a Bourke.'

'Not yet,' Ethan had chuckled.

So Victoria and her grand plans were ignored because the wedding of Summer Dalton and Ethan Bourke was already arranged to take place in Karingal Park gardens.

So it was no surprise then that it was a small affair, with only family and close friends. The CWA ladies took responsibility for the home cooked catering of finger food on trestle tables, the edges of their pristine white cloths fluttering in the light breeze that drifted across the garden. White origami doves and bio-degradable paper chains were hung and looped everywhere overhead from the lowest of the broad sprawling branches of the ancient shady trees, now burning with autumn colour.

Victoria, of course, stood resplendent in a designer tea gown and sweeping elegant mesh hat beside Eleanor Bates, comfortable in a far less fashionable long striped cotton dress. She and David had returned to the district for the first time since leaving over two decades before.

Myrtle Pearce stood alongside Sam Guthrie, leaning on his walking cane, his nostalgic gaze into the distance, perhaps remembering years gone by and his love lost.

Jean and Red Miller were seated next to Corey Sanderson and their daughter, Sally, who was now wearing a small, glittering diamond on her left hand and a huge, happy smile on her face.

Ivy, toddling ahead of her mother, insisted on carrying Misty the kitten in her basket of rose petals from Summer's garden, her dark hair streaming down her back between the wings of her purple fairy costume.

The bride looked dreamy in a soft cream dress that flowed over her slender body, her hair braided and entwined with flowers and ribbons, long crystal earrings glittering in the late afternoon sunlight.

Summer melted at the sight of her dangerously handsome fiancé in a cream suit and casual open-necked shirt, waiting beside the celebrant ahead as she slowly walked toward him on David's arm, beaming.

She didn't need a certificate or piece of paper to know that she and this strong, gorgeous man would walk positively and happily through life together, but they both agreed they wanted it as a public pledge of their love and commitment.

When Summer reached Ethan, he whispered, 'Hi,' and slid an arm possessively around her waist, pressing her against him before taking the liberty of a sweet kiss.

'Don't be greedy,' Summer whispered, blushing.

'I can't wait.' Then to the grinning local marriage celebrant, he added, 'Hurry up, Grace. We want to make this legal.'

THE END

MELTWATER

Della Galton

When Nina's husband, Carl, dies in a skiing accident she feels that she'll never recover. Carl's twin sister, Ingrid, persuades Nina not to sell the riding stables that she and Carl built up. But whilst the horses help her through the grief — Nina's heart is still frozen. Then along comes Oliver, a motherless child, who communicates far better with horses than people. Nina teaches Oliver to ride but can Oliver and his father, Stewart, teach Nina to live again?

HEARTS IN EXILE

Catriona McCuaig

Two teachers are evacuated from Coventry to the Welsh countryside, where they struggle with wartime hardship as they help their pupils adjust to a different way of life. Will love follow them there? Vivacious Tansy sees marriage as a way to escape her impoverished background, while shy Dinah just wants to find someone to love. She falls for handsome Emlyn, but the young Welshman is equally reserved. How will they ever get together?